By Choi Gyu-seok

2

Volume 2

Story Advisors:
Ha Jong-gang, Kim Kyeong-wook, Lee Seon-ok

Art Assistance:
Jeong Pil-won

Foreign Language Dialogue Supervision:
Kim Nak-ho

Chapter2
(Continued)

AFTER THE STORE MANAGER'S IMPRESSIVE WAR DECLARATION, I OFFICIALLY BECAME AN OUTCAST.

SUCH CLEAR MESSAGES FROM COMMANDERS REDUCE THE MENTAL BURDEN ON SOLDIERS AND ENCOURAGE PURPOSEFUL BEHAVIOR.

EXACTLY AS INTENDED, THEY ATTACKED AND ISOLATED ME AS THOUGH IT WERE PART OF THEIR NORMAL WORKFLOW.

HOWEVER, THE MANAGER'S MESSAGE HAD THE SAME EFFECT ON ME.

콰직
THUD
SINCE IT'S BEEN MADE CLEAR THAT THERE'S NO CAMARADERIE HERE, THERE'S NO REASON TO PRETEND.
BANG
콰당

I TOLD YOU NOT TO DO THE DISPLAYS YOURSELF, DIDN'T I?!
WHY ARE YOU STILL WEARING AN APRON?!
...
WHAT ELSE AM I SUPPOSED TO DO WHEN WE'RE SHORT-STAFFED?
...
IF YOU DON'T LIKE YOUR MANAGER WEARING A FLOOR APRON, HIRE MORE PEOPLE.
IF YOU KNOW YOU WON'T GET ANY FAVORS IN RETURN, YOU DON'T HAVE TO PUT ON A SHOW.

NO JOKE. SOMEONE'S JUST QUIT AT THE SALAD BAR, TOO.
I GET WHAT YOU'RE SAYING, BUT...
...I'M SCARED...
ALL THE MORE REASON TO SIGN UP.
BEING UNIONIZED MAKES IT HARDER FOR THEM TO FIRE YOU.
MR. LEE, WHAT ARE YOU DOING?
OH!

DOWN!
WHA... HERE?
EH...?
ISN'T IT KINDA SHITTY?

GENTLEMAN!
DID YOU NOT HEAR ME?
GET DOWN NOW!!
촤 SPLISH
촤 SPLISH
촤 SPLISH
촤 SPLISH
촤 SPLISH
UH...!
UGH!
철벅 SPLASH
QUICKLY!!

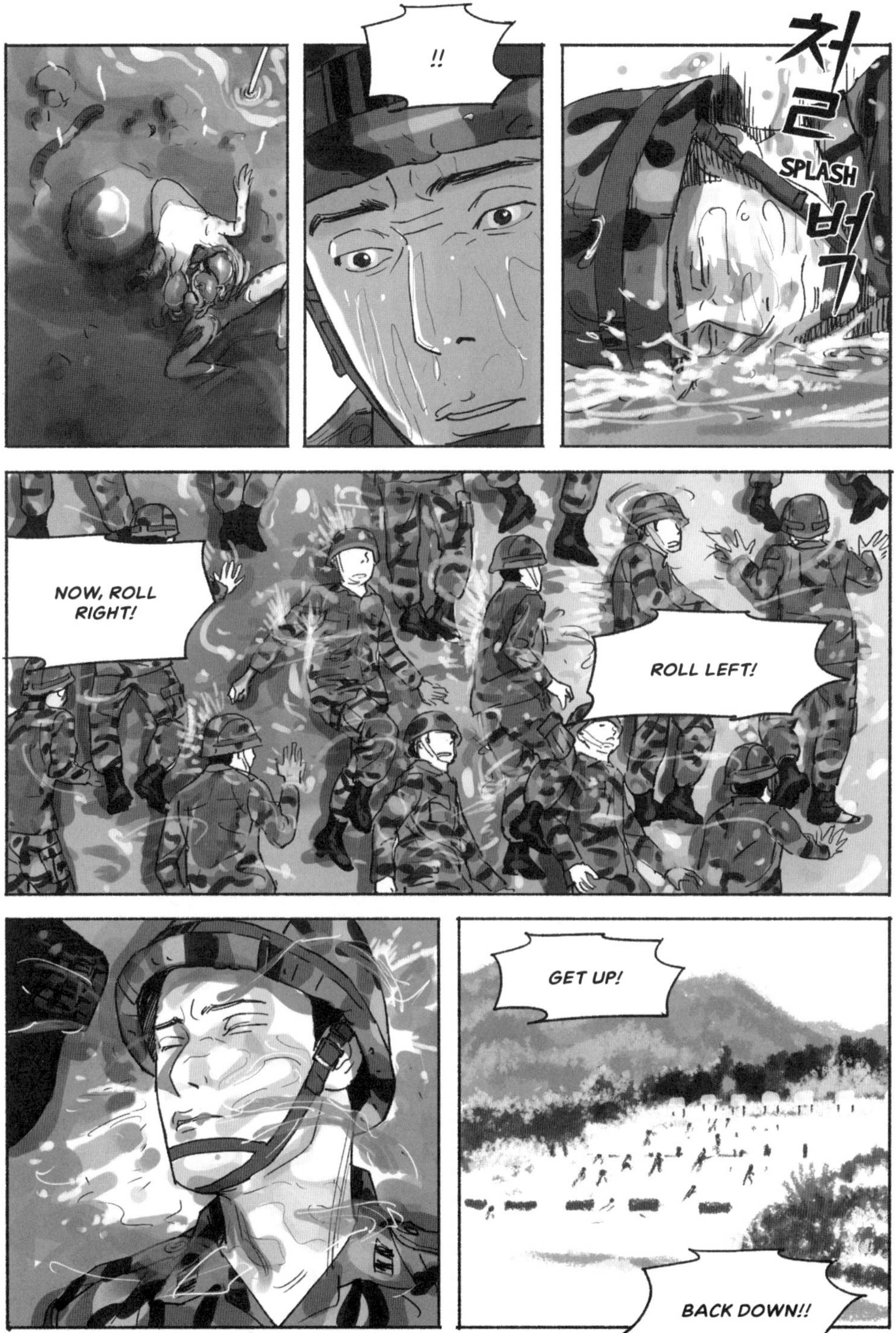
!!
철벅
SPLASH
NOW, ROLL RIGHT!
ROLL LEFT!
GET UP!
BACK DOWN!!

UP!!
AFTER SWALLOWING A MOUTHFUL OF THAT RANCID WATER AND GETTING SOAKED THROUGH TO MY UNDERWEAR IN IT, I FELT A STRANGE SENSE OF LIBERATION.
IT MADE ME SOMEHOW NOT CARE ABOUT CRAWLING ON THE ROUGH GROUND, MOUTH FULL OF DUST...
...OR GETTING JABBED AND SCRATCHED UP HERE AND THERE.

MR. LEE, CAN'T YOU HEAR ME?
WHAT ARE YOU DOING?
ME?
I'M ENCOURAGING OUR EMPLOYEES TO JOIN THE UNION.

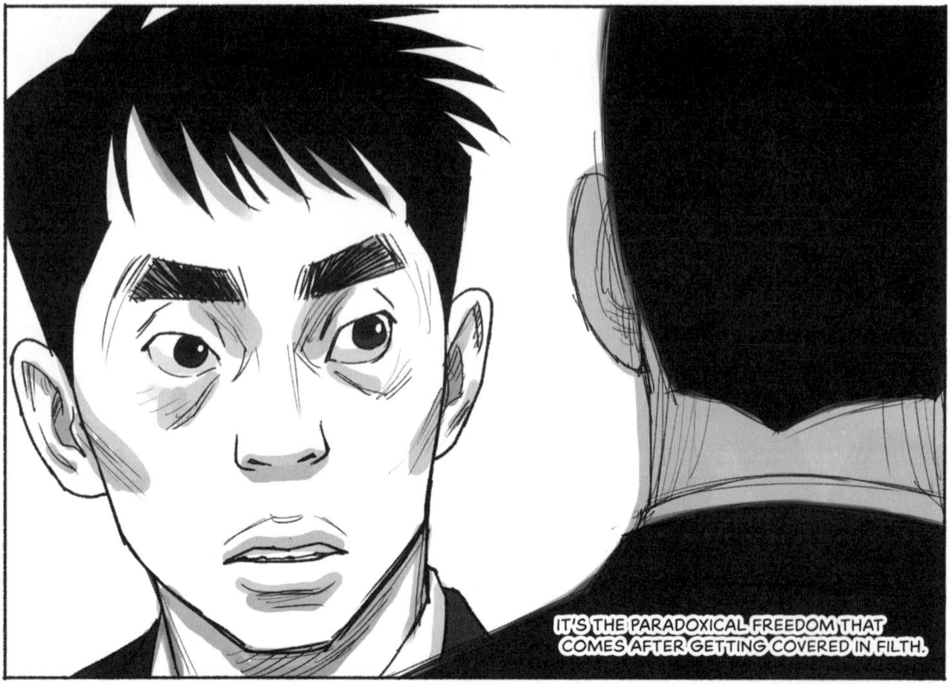
IT'S THE PARADOXICAL FREEDOM THAT
COMES AFTER GETTING COVERED IN FILTH.

I FEEL LIKE... I WAS TRULY MADE TO BE AN OUTCAST.

SAY THERE'S AN UMBRELLA FACTORY AND A FAN FACTORY...
...AND EACH OF THE TWO FACTORIES EMPLOYS TEN CRAFTSMEN FULL-TIME.
THERE'S A RAINY SEASON AND A DRY SEASON HERE. NATURALLY, UMBRELLAS SELL WELL IN THE RAINY SEASON AND FANS IN THE DRY SEASON.
BUT WITH ONLY TEN PEOPLE, THEY CAN'T MEET DEMANDS. SO THERE'S A SHORTAGE OF UMBRELLAS IN THE RAINY SEASON AND FANS IN THE DRY SEASON.
CONVERSELY, THERE'S AN EXCESS OF WORKERS AT EACH FACTORY DURING THEIR RESPECTIVE OFF-SEASONS.
BECAUSE OF THIS, BOTH FACTORIES AGREE TO SEND FIVE EMPLOYEES FROM THE EXCESS FACTORY TO THE SHORTAGE FACTORY.
THAT WAY, THE EMPLOYEES ARE NEVER IN A STATE OF TOO MUCH OR TOO LITTLE WORK, AND THE FACTORIES BOTH BENEFIT.
CONSUMERS ARE ABLE TO GET WHAT THEY WANT ON TIME, AND SOCIETY AS A WHOLE IS MORE PRODUCTIVE.

THAT'S LABOR FLEXIBILITY. GET IT?
IF THERE'S A NEED FOR MANPOWER, IT'S EASY TO HIRE SOMEONE...
...AND IT'S EASY TO CUT THEM WHEN THE WORK'S LOW.
THIS IS GOOD FOR YOUR SISTER, GOOD FOR YOUR BROTHER-IN-LAW, AND GOOD FOR SOCIETY AS A WHOLE, RIGHT?
GOING BACK TO OUR TWO FACTORIES... WHO IN THAT SITUATION IS ENTITLED TO THE EXTRA PROFIT GENERATED?
THE WORKERS WHO GO BACK-AND-FORTH BETWEEN THE FACTORIES, RIGHT?
THOSE BACK-AND-FORTH GUYS REPRESENT OUR REAL-WORLD TEMP WORKERS. DISPATCHED LABOR.
TEMP WORK IS ROUGH. YOU HAVE TO CONSTANTLY LEARN NEW SKILLS, MOVE AROUND, AND SPEND LENGTHY PERIODS BETWEEN RELIABLE JOBS...
THIS IS WHY IT MAKES SENSE FOR TEMP WORKERS TO HAVE A HIGHER SALARY.

BUT WHAT'S COMMON PRACTICE IN REALITY?
DISPATCHED WORKERS GET PAID LESS, RIGHT? HALF THE FULL-TIME WAGE IN THE WORST CASES.
SO, BUSINESSES ARE MAKING MORE MONEY BECAUSE OF CONTINGENT WORKERS, BUT THE OVERALL LABOR COSTS ARE GOING DOWN? WHERE DOES THAT MONEY GO?
THE COMPANY GETS IT.
SURE, BUT THERE'S MORE TO IT THAN THAT.
SO? WHO ELSE BENEFITS?
THE GUY WITH THE FLAG.
THE MIDDLEMAN TAKES HIS SHARE.
PLACEMENT AGENCIES ADVERTISING DISPATCHED WORK OR SUBCONTRACTING OR WHATEVER...
YOU NEED TEN PEOPLE BY MONDAY?
...MOVE PEOPLE FROM COMPANY TO COMPANY WITH A SINGLE PHONE.
WHAT'S THE DIFFERENCE BETWEEN THIS AND A FEUDAL FARM SUPERVISOR?
HEY, CAN'T YOU HOE PROPERLY? DO YOU WANT TO BE EVICTED?

* ABOUT $222 USD AT CURRENT CONVERSION RATE (2024)

IN 2002, 70 PERCENT OF NEW HIRES WERE DISPATCHED WORKERS.
SO, IF THESE PEOPLE WORK HARD, DO THEY GET A FULL-TIME JOB?
THE ODDS OF TRANSITIONING TO A FULL-TIME POSITION AFTER FOUR YEARS IS LESS THAN 9 PERCENT.
IN THE U.S., CONTRACT WORKERS HAVE A 57 PERCENT CHANCE OF BECOMING FULL-TIME EMPLOYEES AFTER ONE YEAR.
WHAT DOES THIS MEAN?
WHAT DOES THAT TELL YOU?
THIS MEANS THAT WORKERS IN KOREA HAVE VERY LITTLE HOPE FOR A SECURE CAREER, EVEN IF THEY WORK HARD THEIR ENTIRE LIVES.
AND THIS ISN'T A RECENT PHENOMENON.
IN 1997, WHEN THE IMF* BAILOUT HAPPENED, AND PEOPLE WERE HANDING OVER THEIR GOLD TO SAVE THE COUNTRY, HANDING IN THEIR RESIGNATIONS TO SAVE THEIR COMPANIES...
* INTERNATIONAL MONETARY FUND

EVEN IF IT WAS CHAOS, YOU'D EXPECT THINGS TO GO BACK TO THE WAY THEY USED TO BE ONCE THE ECONOMY IMPROVED, RIGHT?
IN THOSE DAYS, A SINGLE INCOME COULD SUPPORT A FAMILY AND PUT YOUR KIDS THROUGH SCHOOL.
BUT THOSE DAYS AREN'T COMING BACK.
WHAT KIND OF MADMAN WOULD WANT TO CHANGE A WORLD WHERE YOU CAN USE PEOPLE AS MUCH AS YOU WANT AND THEN DISPOSE OF THEM WHENEVER YOU WANT, EASY AS TURNING A TAP ON AND OFF?
GIVE IT A FEW MORE YEARS, AND YOU WON'T EVEN REMEMBER THOSE DAYS EXISTED.

OH, BOSS.

GOD, YOU'RE HOPELESS!
YOU'RE UNPOPULAR WITH YOUR EMPLOYEES, RIGHT? SO WHO'S GOING TO LISTEN TO YOU?
YOU HAVE TO PINPOINT WHO THEY LIKE AND TRUST, AND THEN GO AFTER THAT PERSON FIRST!
WHEN I WAS IN THE MILITARY, I WAS A PLATOON LEADER WITH A COUPLE OF DISTINCTIONS, AND I HAD GOOD LEADERSHIP SKILLS...
AND WHO ASKED YOU TO LEAD THEM?
JUST PERFORMING THE ROUTINE DOESN'T MAKE YOU A LEADER.
THIS ISN'T A GROUP CONSCRIPTED BY THE STATE WHO'LL BE PUNISHED IF THEY RUN AWAY.
YOU HAVE TO RECRUIT PEOPLE YOURSELF, AND IF THEY DESERT, THAT'S THAT.
FIND SOMEONE CHARISMATIC. IT'LL GO FASTER.

WE KEEP BUMPING INTO EACH OTHER TODAY, HUH, MR. LEE?
AH... YEAH, I GUESS SO.
WELL, I'M HEADING BACK OUT.
OH, UH... WAIT, MR. JU.
YES, SIR?
UH...
GO AHEAD.
I JUST THOUGHT...
...UNION AND...
...DO YOU WANT TO JOIN?
OH... I DIDN'T HEAR YOU, SO...

UN...ION.
DO YOU WANT TO JOIN THE UNION?

JOON-CHEOL, CAN'T YOU COME IN ON YOUR OFF DAY? I'LL NEVER ASK AGAIN!
I REALLY CAN'T, BOSS.
IF I BREAK MY PROMISE AGAIN, MIN-JEONG WILL KILL ME.
C'MON...
YOU CAN TREAT HER THE NEXT TIME YOU HAVE A DAY OFF.
I JUST HEARD OLIVIER, THE HEAD OF OPERATIONS, IS COMING. I CAN'T FACE HIM WITHOUT YOU.
HM? HELP ME OUT, BROTHER.
BUT... I REALLY CAN'T...
HEY! CAN'T WE ACCOMPLISH ANYTHING WORKING TOGETHER?
YOU WANT DRINKS AND FOOD TONIGHT? I'LL PAY! WHAT DO YOU WANT? SASHIMI?

IF SHE BREAKS UP WITH ME, I'M HOLDING YOU RESPONSIBLE.
THAT'S FINE BY ME. HOW SHOULD I REPENT? SHOULD I FILE FOR DIVORCE?
GROSS... DON'T TOUCH ME...
WHY NOT? I'M TAKING RESPONSIBILITY.
SOO-IN LEE... YOU DON'T HAVE A FRIENDLY RELATIONSHIP WITH YOUR EMPLOYEES, DO YOU?
2002/2003Y Labor cost by Division
esh Fast Food / Salad Bar 200,765,067 178,645,381
esh Fish 167,245,204 149,889,834
esh Fruits & Vegetables 245,537,611 246,335,444
esh Bakery Pastery 221,938,918 187,079,624
esh Butchery 175,416,953 155,260,968
zaar D.I.Y 21,770,383 25,071,364
zaar Housekeeping 113,864,811 127,211,904
zaar Culture Stationery 63,507,535 67,961,224
zaar Leisure 108,364,308 114,018,028
zaar Gardening 7,534,028 13,115,944
zaar Cars 47,297,404 64,319,828
콰
THUD
THIS IS YOUR TARGET!

SLOW! SLOW! WAY TOO SLOW!
HOW CAN I KEEP TRUSTING YOU?
I'M... SORRY, GASTON. I'M DO... MY BEST.
IS THAT ALL YOU CAN SAY? I DON'T NEED YOUR BEST.
I NEED RESULTS.
DO YOU HAVE AN ACTUAL PLAN?
UH... I'M NO LOOKING... FOR...

STOP!
I'VE BEEN HERE FOR YEARS! WHY DON'T YOU SPEAK ENGLISH?
GET OUT!

MR. HEO...
HAVE YOU SEEN THE FLYER ITEM LIST?
I THINK MR. JEONG HAD IT PULLED UP...

EGARD TO
DD DEPARTMENT REPORT
NY SELECTION CRITERIA
ONS
TAK
TA
DAK
CLICK
CLICK
틱 틱 틱 . . .
TIK TIK TIK

위이이이이
WRRRRRRRR
이이이이잉
RRRRR
잉
RRR
잉
RRR
잉
RRR
RRR
잉

RRR
AH!
RRR
PRIIINT
RRR
RRR...
• • •
WHAT ARE YOU DOING AT MY DESK?
AH...
I WAS LOOKING FOR THE LIST OF SALE ITEMS.

WELL, IT'S
NOT HERE.

Café C
ARE YOU KIDDING ME?!
DIDN'T YOU SAY YOU HAD TIME OFF?!
HEY, KEEP YOUR VOICE DOWN.
WHAT KIND OF COMPANY HAS TO SWAP SHIFTS AROUND SO MUCH? EVEN PART-TIME WORK ISN'T THIS WISHY-WASHY.
I ALREADY MADE RESERVATIONS, SO WHAT I AM SUPPOSED TO DO?!
YOU JUST HAVEN'T WORKED A COMPANY JOB YET. THIS IS JUST WHAT IT'S LIKE.
IF SOMETHING COMES UP AND THE PERSON WHO CAN TAKE CARE OF IT ISN'T THERE, WHAT HAPPENS?
DO YOU THINK THE STORE SHOULD CLOSE?
NO, BUT WHY IS THAT PERSON ALWAYS YOU?
THEY'RE TAKING ADVANTAGE OF YOU, THAT'S WHY!
DO YOU THINK IT WAS EASY FOR ME TO FIGURE OUT MY SCHEDULE JUST BECAUSE I WORK PART-TIME? I BARELY MANAGED IT!

THE MANAGER SAID HE COULDN'T DO IT WITHOUT ME. WHAT WAS I SUPPOSED TO DO?
IF THEY KEEP ASKING ME TO TAKE CARE OF THINGS, IT'S BECAUSE I'M GOOD AT WHAT I DO. DON'T YOU WANT ME TO HAVE A JOB?
BUT ISN'T IT THE SAME MANAGER WHO KEEPS TORMENTING YOU?
NO, IT'S ALL THAT ASSHOLE JEONG'S FAULT...
DO YOU THINK KYEONG-SIK LIKES DOING THIS?
HE'S LOOKING OUT FOR ME.
HE ALWAYS ASKS ME TO WORK BECAUSE HE WANTS ME TO LEARN.
THEY ONLY DO IT BECAUSE YOU CAN'T SAY NO TO THEM. BUT WHAT ABOUT ME?
IT'S NOT THAT BIG OF A DEAL.

HEY... MIN-JEONG...
WHAT ARE YOU...
WHAT ARE
YOU SAYING?

I TRIED TO STOP IT, BUT YOU KNOW HOW THE COMPANY IS THESE DAYS...
IF YOU WRITE A LETTER OF RESIGNATION, I'LL MAKE SURE YOU GET TWO EXTRA MONTHS OF COMPENSATION.
IF YOU'RE FIRED FOR DISCIPLINARY ACTION, YOU WON'T RECEIVE UNEMPLOYMENT BENEFITS.
WRITE THE LETTER BEFORE IT'S TOO LATE.

WHAT ABOUT YOU? YOU WERE THERE, TOO!
WHY AM I THE ONLY ONE GETTING IN TROUBLE?
HOW SHOULD I KNOW? ONLY YOUR NAME CAME UP.
DO YOU REALLY WANT ME TO GET FIRED, TOO?

YOU WENT OUT THAT NIGHT BECAUSE KYEONG-SIK INVITED YOU.
SO WHY IS IT YOUR FAULT?
CAB FARE...
WHEN WE PARTED WAYS, MR. KIM GAVE ME MONEY FOR A TAXI...
BRO, DO YOU THINK KYEONG-SIK IS TRYING TO GET YOU FIRED?
NO... KYEONG-SIK CAN BE A BIT OF A JERK, BUT HE WOULDN'T DO THAT...
HEY, SHUT UP! IT'S MY BOSS.
YES, SIR.

MR. JU, ARE YOU CLOSE WITH JOON-CHEOL HWANG FROM THE FISH DEPARTMENT?
AH, YES... WE'RE TOGETHER RIGHT NOW...
DO YOU HAPPEN TO KNOW IF EVERYTING IS OKAY WITH HIM?
?
...
HOW... HOW DO...?
DID HE WRITE A RESIGNATION LETTER?!
A RESIGNATION LETTER?
NO... NOT YET.
HUH? YOU'RE COMING?

According to an anonymous tip, employee Joon-cheol Hwang of Fresh Seafood Department, stated that at 8:00pm on Wednesda May 28, 2003, he attended a karaoke bar with employees of Yeonggwang Fisheries Co., LTD., and received a bribe from CEO Bok-seong Kim.
DID...
...DID MY MANAGER WRITE THIS?
YES.
I...
...I CAN'T BELIEVE THIS.

쾅
BANG
JOON-CHEOL!
THAT BASTARD IS AT IT AGAIN...
쾅
BANG
STOP IT! YOU'RE BLEEDING!

쾅
BANG
HEY, JOON-CHEOL! STOP IT!
JOON-CHEOL...
YOU KNOW WHAT?
I DIDN'T SAY ANYTHING BECAUSE I WAS EMBARRASSED, BUT...
LAST YEAR, ON MIN-JEONG'S BIRTHDAY...
...I WAS BLOWING UP BALLOONS AND PUTTING CANDLES ON THE CAKE TO HELP WITH HIS MARRIAGE PROPOSAL.
THIS TIME WE WERE SUPPOSED TO GO ON VACATION...
MIN-JEONG COULDN'T WAIT, BUT THAT BASTARD...

WE HAVE TO MAKE HIM PAY!
LET'S MAKE A SCENE AT WORK, AND THEN ALL QUIT AT THE SAME TIME!
IF WE ALL LEAVE, THAT'LL BE TROUBLE FOR HIM!
YEAH, IF YOU GET FIRED, THEN WE'LL ALL QUIT.
SHOULD I CALL MR. HEO NOW?
EVERYBODY, TAKE A MINUTE AND TRY TO CALM DOWN.
THIS IS NONE OF YOUR BUSINESS!
HOW CAN WE STAY CALM?
DO YOU KNOW HOW MANY YEARS MR. HEO AND JOON-CHEOL HAVE KNOWN EACH OTHER?
FIVE YEARS!

THAT BASTARD CAN'T DO THIS TO JOON-CHEOL!
MIN-HO, DO YOU REALLY NEED TO BE SO DISRESPECTFUL TOWARD MR. HEO?
BUT IT'S TRUE...
CHEOL-MIN JEONG, IS THERE A PROBLEM?
WHY ARE YOU ALL GATHERED AT THIS HOUR?
NO PROBLEM HERE, SIR.
I DIDN'T THINK SO. GET OUT OF THE WAY.
LET'S GET BACK INSIDE, EVERYONE.
턱
THUD

THINGS ARE GOING TO BE PICKING UP SOON, SO THE IDEAL TIME TO RESIGN IS WHEN EVERYONE IS BUSIEST...
THAT'S A GOOD IDEA.
WHERE DID YOU LEARN TO BE SO DUMB?
YOUR COWORKER IS ABOUT TO GET HIS HEAD CUT OFF...
...SO YOU'RE THINKING ABOUT GETTING YOURS CUT OFF, TOO?
YOU'RE A BUNCH OF MODEL EMPLOYEES!

THEY'RE COMING FOR YOU ONE BY ONE BECAUSE IT'S HARD TO GET RID OF EVERYONE ALL AT ONCE.
THEY'LL BE GLAD TO WATCH YOU LEAVE IN SINGLE FILE. THANK YOU VERY MUCH! MERCI BEAUCOUP!
...
BUT...
DO YOU THINK THE COMPANY HATES YOU?
DO YOU THINK YOU'RE THAT IMPORTANT?
RIGHT NOW, 77% OF SUPERMARKET EMPLOYEES ARE TEMP WORKERS.
AND THE AVERAGE TENURE IS LESS THAN 3 YEARS...
AND FOURMIS?
33% OF EMPLOYEES ARE FULL-TIME, ON PAR WITH OTHER COMPANIES.
THEY'RE TRYING TO GET RID OF YOU AND REPLACE YOU WITH TEMP WORKERS...
...TO SAVE MONEY. GET IT YET?

IF YOU WANT TO FIGHT BACK, YOU HAVE TO HIT THEM WHERE IT HURTS. NOT TICKLE THEM.
YOU HAVE TO REEEEALLY LOVE THE COMPANY.
WHAT SHOULD WE DO?
YOU NEED TO SHOW THEM HOW TOUGH YOU ARE.
FIRST, LET'S LOOK AT THE FOURMIS EMPLOYEE HANDBOOK.
WHAT'S THE EMPLOYEE HANDBOOK?
HUH? HOW DOES A MANAGER NOT KNOW WHAT THAT IS?
IT HAS ALL OF THE COMPANY POLICIES AND PROCEDURES.
WHY DO WE NEED THAT?
BECAUSE YOU HAVE TO KNOW THE RULES TO PLAY THE GAME, RIGHT?

EXCUSE ME, CAN YOU GIVE ME A COPY OF THE EMPLOYEE HANDBOOK?
WHAT... WHY?
WHY NOT?
SHOULDN'T EVERYONE BE ABLE TO READ IT?
I GUESS SO...?
MR. PARK, WHERE'S OUR EMPLOYEE HANDBOOK?
WHAT'S THAT?

HMM...
...I THINK I SAW IT IN HERE SOMEWHERE...
IS THAT...?
AH, THERE IT IS!
HERE IT IS.
Employee Handbook
I THOUGHT EMPLOYMENT RULES WERE SUPPOSED TO BE POSTED OR PLACED SO THAT ALL EMPLOYEES CAN SEE THEM?
...
WELL... IT'S "PLACED" HERE IN THIS CABINET...

I'LL PUT IT THIS WAY... IT HAS EVERYTHING IT'S SUPPOSED TO.
BUT, LIKE I FIGURED, IT'S BETTER TO PUT IT BACK WHERE YOU FOUND IT.
WHY?
THEY'RE ALL JUST EMPTY WORDS COPIED FROM OTHER MANUALS.
IF THEY'RE SMART, NOW THAT YOU'VE STARTED MAKING MOVES, THEY'LL TRY TO FIRE YOU TO PROTECT THEMSELVES.
WE'LL TRY TO CHALLENGE THEM DURING THE DISCIPLINARY HEARING.
YEAH...

WHAT IS THIS? THERE'RE TOO MANY STRANGE LOOKING THINGS THESE DAYS.
I THINK IT'S TO LAY BACK ON.
IS THIS SUPPOSED TO BE A WORKOUT?
HUH?!
OH...
OH...

UH UH UH UH UH
S... SOO-IN...
SOO-IN...
HELP...

WHOA...
ARE YOU OKAY? YOU SHOULD SEE A DOCTOR.
NO. I JUST GOT SCARED.
I'M OLD. I'M JUST... OLD.

WHAT'S THAT FACE ABOUT?
WERE YOU AFRAID I WAS GOING TO DIE?
I WAS THINKING ABOUT MR. HWANG...
JOON-CHEOL?
MR. HEO MAY HAVE INVITED HIM, BUT HE DIDN'T REFUSE...
MAYBE IT WASN'T THE ONLY TIME THAT HAPPENED...
SO?
WHAT ARE YOU TRYING TO SAY?
THAT COMPANIES SHOULD BE ABLE TO FIRE ANYONE WHO ISN'T AS SQUEAKY CLEAN AS YOU?

OH... NO... THAT'S NOT WHAT I MEANT.
BUT GOING TO A PLACE LIKE THAT WHEN HE HAS A GIRLFRIEND...
SO?
SOO-IN, KEEP THIS IN MIND...
YOU'RE NOT PROTECTING JOON-CHEOL HWANG, BUT A HUMAN BEING.
NOT A PURE AND KIND PERSON.
JUST A COWARDLY, MISERABLE, AND INSIGNIFICANT HUMAN BEING.

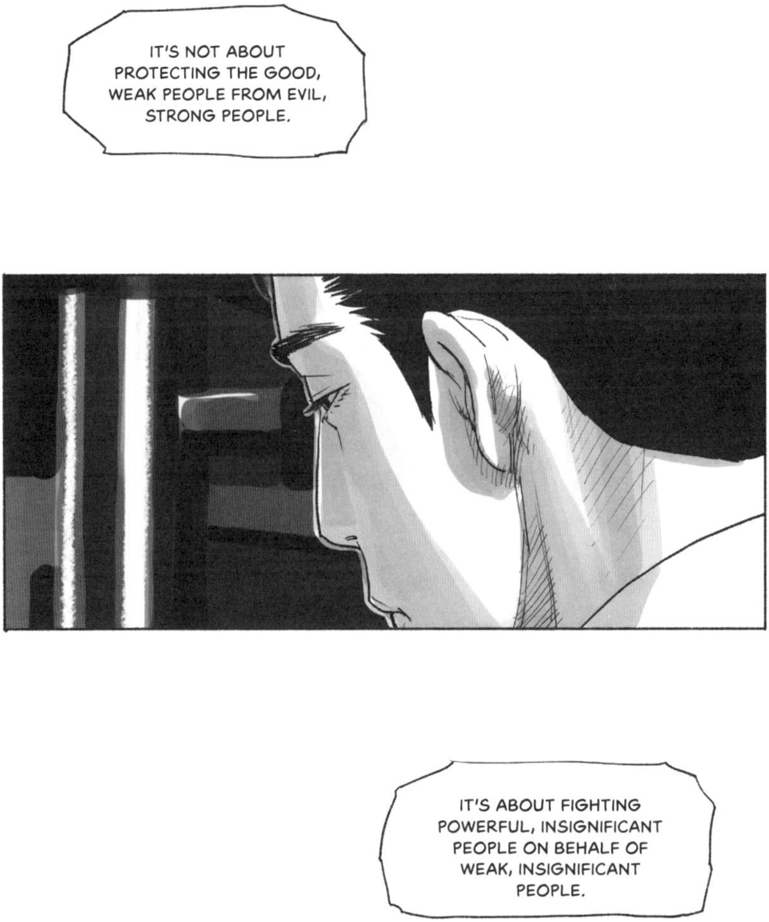
IT'S NOT ABOUT PROTECTING THE GOOD, WEAK PEOPLE FROM EVIL, STRONG PEOPLE.
IT'S ABOUT FIGHTING POWERFUL, INSIGNIFICANT PEOPLE ON BEHALF OF WEAK, INSIGNIFICANT PEOPLE.

WHY HAVEN'T YOU SUBMITTED A RESIGNATION LETTER?
IF YOU DON'T DO IT SOON, I WON'T BE ABLE TO COVER FOR YOU ANYMORE.
IF YOU DON'T DO IT, YOU'LL BE DISCIPLINED AND FIRED.
THAT'S NOT GOOD FOR YOU. IT'LL MAKE GETTING ANOTHER JOB DIFFICULT.
THEY'LL KEEP ASKING YOU TO RESIGN.
DON'T DO IT. IF YOU DO, YOU CAN'T TAKE IT BACK.
DON'T SIGN ANYTHING THE COMPANY ASKS YOU TO, WHETHER IT'S A RESIGNATION LETTER OR SOMETHING ELSE.
THEY DON'T ASK FOR SIGNATURES ON ANYTHING THAT WORKS IN OUR FAVOR.
ANYTHING THE COMPANY WANTS US TO SIGN IS GOING TO WORK AGAINST US.

THAT'S RIGHT! EMPLOYEE CONSENT IS ONLY NEEDED IF THE CHANGE IS UNFAVORABLE TO THEM.
I WENT FROM A FULL-TIME EMPLOYEE TO A PART-TIME ONE OVERNIGHT BECAUSE I MADE THE MISTAKE OF SIGNING SOMETHING, SO I KNOW WHAT IT'S LIKE.
I THOUGHT IT WOULD BE FINE BECAUSE THE UNION SAID IT WAS OKAY. WHAT DID I KNOW?
DARE THEM TO FIRE YOU.
DIDN'T YOU SAY YOU WERE READY TO RESIGN? NOW YOU DON'T WANT TO GET FIRED?
WHAT... WHAT IF I ACTUALLY GET FIRED?
IF YOU GET FIRED, I'LL TAKE ON YOUR CASE FOR FREE. THERE'S JUST NO GUARANTEE I'LL WIN!
JUST... TELL THEM TO FIRE ME.
WHAT'S WRONG WITH YOU, MAN? SEVERANCE AND UNEMPLOYMENT MONEY ARE NOTHING TO SNEEZE AT.
WHY ARE YOU TRYING TO LOSE MONEY?

THEY ASKED YOU THAT BULLSHIT?!
DO YOU KNOW WHAT HAPPENS IF YOU SUBMIT YOUR RESIGNATION AND DECIDE TO LEAVE?
YOU WON'T GET ANY UNEMPLOYMENT BENEFITS.
BUT IF YOU'RE FIRED AND IT'S DECIDED YOU WERE UNFAIRLY DISMISSED, YOU GET COMPENSATED FOR THE MISSED WORKDAYS.
YOU DON'T WORK, YOU SPEND YOUR TIME HOW YOU WANT, AND YOU GET PAID. IT'S ALL GOOD!
THINK CAREFULLY.
THINK ABOUT ALL THE EFFORT I'VE PUT INTO YOUR CAREER...
I'M SORRY THIS IS CAUSING YOU SO MUCH TROUBLE.
HUH?

INSTEAD OF GOING THROUGH ALL THE TROUBLE, JUST TELL THEM TO DISCIPLINE ME.
WHEN THE DISCIPLINARY COMMITTEE IS CALLED, I'LL GO.
HAS THE COMPANY EVER HELD A DISCIPLINARY COMMITTEE?
I DON'T THINK SO.
REALLY? THEN THEY'LL SURELY MAKE SOME MISSTEPS.
AND THAT'S WHEN WE STRIKE.
JOON-CHEOL HWANG.
HERE IS THE DISCIPLINARY COMMITTE ATTENDANCE NOTICE.

THE EMPLOYMENT RULES STATE YOU MUST GIVE THREE DAYS ADVANCE NOTICE FOR THE DISCIPLINARY COMMITTEE.
THIS IS TOMORROW'S DATE.
PLEASE FOLLOW THE RULES AND ISSUE ANOTHER NOTIFICATION.
O... OKAY...

DID YOU SEE THAT?
부진노동상담소*
KANG-MIN, YOU SHOULD HAVE SEEN KYUNG-SIK'S FACE!
*LABOR COUNSELING CENTER
YOU KNOW THE FACE A KID MAKES WHEN THEY GET SCOLDED?
STOP! YOU'VE BEEN TALKING ABOUT IT NON-STOP ALL DAY.
HR WAS WORKING OVERTIME TO PREPARE FOR THE MEETING.
DID YOU SEE IT, TOO, BOSS?
YEAH... I THINK WE MADE A FEW ENEMIES AT HEADQUARTERS.
IT'S OKAY. THE PRODUCE DEPARTMENT IS GOING STRONG!
AS LONG AS WE'RE IN THIS TOGETHER, IT'S GAME OVER FOR THE BIG GUYS!
HEO MUST BE IN HOT WATER WITH THE STORE MANAGER. IT DOESN'T GET MUCH WORSE FOR HIM THAN THAT.
HAHA... YEAH...
WHO DO YOU THINK YOU ARE?
HUBRIS, MAN! HAHA.

SORRY, CHIEF.
WHY'S THAT?
I KNOW YOU AREN'T REALLY CLOSE WITH THE EMPLOYEES...
BUT YOU STILL DECIDED TO BE ON OUR SIDE.
YOU WERE THERE FOR JOON-CHEOL...
NO.
I DIDN'T DO ANYTHING.
SO... I HAD A PRIVATE MEETING WITH MR. JEONG THE OTHER DAY.

HEY, KANG-MIN. SOO-IN LEE'S ON HIS WAY OUT.
YOU KNOW YOU'LL BE THE ONE TO TAKE HIS PLACE, RIGHT?
I'M STILL YOUNG...
HEY, THE CHANGWON BRANCH HAS A 24-YEAR-OLD MANAGER. YOU'RE NOT TOO YOUNG. IT'S ALL ABOUT HOW MUCH EXPERIENCE YOU HAVE.
HONESTLY, DOES THE PRODUCE DEPARTMENT LISTEN TO YOU OR TO MR. LEE?
RIGHT NOW, YOU'RE GOING TO HAVE TO TAKE CARE OF YOUR EMPLOYEES AND NOT GET INVOLVED WITH MR. LEE.
YOU KNOW WHAT I MEAN, RIGHT? DRINK UP!
ACTUALLY... I GOT A LITTLE EXCITED.
BUT THAT'S NOT WHY I DIDN'T JOIN THE UNION...

IT'S A BIT SCARY...
IT ALSO SOUNDS LIKE A REAL HASSLE, AND...
YOU... YOU AREN'T ANGRY?
THEY ORDERED ME TO LAY EVERYONE OFF THREE WEEKS AGO...
...AND I'VE BEEN ANGRY EVER SINCE.
...
CHIEF, YOU'RE A REAL MAN.
I'LL JOIN THE UNION!

OH, REALLY?
KEEP IT DOWN!
FROM NOW ON, I WILL CONSIDER YOU A BROTHER!
AN OLDER BROTHER!
...
NO... THAT'S... UH... A BIT... A BIT TOO MUCH...
NO! I WILL TREAT YOU AS MY BROTHER!
UNION?
IF KANG-MIN'S DOING IT, SO WILL WE!

WE'LL FLIP THE COMPANY UPSIDE DOWN AND SET THE STORE MANAGER'S CAR ON FIRE, RIGHT?
YEAH, SURE. IF YOU WANT TO DESTROY YOUR LIFE.

FISH
SEONG-MIN! WHAT ARE YOU DOING AFTER WORK? WANT TO GET A BEER?
UH... WHY?
DO WE NEED A PARTICULAR REASON?
I HAVE TO GO HOME A LITTLE EARLY TODAY, SO...
...MAYBE NEXT TIME.
WELL, LET'S TALK FOR A SECOND. I HAVE SOMETHING I WANT TO RUN BY YOU.
HEY... LATER. LET'S DO IT LATER.
IT'LL ONLY TAKE A SECOND.
I HAVE TO GO TO THE OFFICE RIGHT NOW.
LET'S TALK ANOTHER TIME. I'M IN A HURRY.

세계로마트*
* WORLD-MART
KYEONG-SIK?
HA... HE'S AN ASSHOLE.
SO WHAT DO YOU WANT?
WHEN YOU WERE AT YEONGGWANG FISHERIES, DID YOU EVER SEE MR. HEO GO OUT WITH GIRLS?
HAHAHA, GO OUT WITH GIRLS? DO YOU KNOW WHAT WE USED TO CALL HIM?
THE LIGHTHOUSE!
HE MAY NOT SEEM LIKE IT, BUT HE'S ALWAYS TURNED ON!
AND HE STAYS ON ALL NIGHT!

ALSO, TELL ME... DID YOU EVER SEE MR. HEO TAKE MONEY FROM ANYONE WITH YEONGGWANG FISHERIES?
I SAW IT A LOT.
I'D SAY ONCE A MONTH.
HEY, SEONG-MIN, WAIT A MINUTE!
JUST WHILE YOU WAIT FOR THE BUS...
OH, WHY? WHAT?
WHEN THE BUS GETS HERE, I HAVE TO GO.

MR. HEO AND JOON-CHEOL HAD DINNER WITH PEOPLE FROM YOUR COMPANY A FEW MONTHS AGO, RIGHT?
A FEW MONTHS AGO? HOW DO YOU REMEMBER THAT?
DON'T YOU KNOW? THE COMPANY IS TRYING TO FIRE JOON-CHEOL BECAUSE OF IT.
I JUST WANT YOU TO WRITE A STATEMENT THAT SAYS MR. HEO WAS ALSO THERE.
SIGH... HE SHOULD PROBABLY JUST QUIT.
WHAT'S THE POINT OF WRITING A STATEMENT?
ISN'T THERE SOMEPLACE ELSE JOON-CHEOL CAN GO WITH HIS KNIFE SKILLS?
DO YOU THINK IT'S FAIR THAT HE'S GOING TO GET FIRED OVER THIS?
HUH? PLEASE JUST WRITE ONE PAGE.
I WANT TO WRITE IT...
BUT IF I DO, WILL FOURMIS CONTINUE TO BUY FISH FROM YEONGGWANG?
WHY DO ALL THIS WHEN YOU KNOW HOW IT ENDS?

THE BUS IS HERE. I HAVE TO GO.
RIIIIING
RIIIIING
RIIIIING
R-I-I-I-I-I-N-G
STILL NOT ANSWERING?
NO...

THE COMPANY PROBABLY CONTACTED HIM AND TOLD HIM NOT TO SPEAK WITH ME...
...
OH?! MR. CHOI!
UH... JOON-CHEOL...
WHAT ARE YOU DOING HERE?
I'VE BEEN TRYING TO REACH YOU.
OH? DID YOU CALL?
JOON-CHEOL, I'M SORRY, BUT I HAVE TO GET INSIDE...
HELLO, MR. CHOI. YOU KNOW ME, RIGHT?
AH... OH, YES, MR. LEE.

YOU'VE BEEN CONTACTED BY FOURMIS, RIGHT?
WE KNOW IT'S A LOT TO ASK, BUT WE'RE BEGGING YOU TO HELP US OUT JUST THIS ONCE.
...
I'M SORRY. PLEASE EXCUSE ME.
SORRY, JOON-CHEOL. LET'S TALK LATER.

* FRIENDS' KARAOKE

IS THERE ANYTHING ELSE WE CAN DO?
I'M STARTING TO WORRY WE WON'T BE ABLE TO GET ENOUGH EVIDENCE...
COULD I ATTEND THE MEETING WITH HIM?
IF YOU WANT, GO AHEAD. NOTHING FORBIDS IT.
BUT DO YOU REALLY THINK IT'LL MAKE A DIFFERENCE?
EVEN IF JOON-CHEOL LOSES, WE CAN ALWAYS APPEAL.
WHAT'S WRONG? YOU LOOK REALLY ANXIOUS.
JOON-CHEOL... DOESN'T REALLY SEEM TO HAVE THE TEMPERAMENT FOR THIS SORT OF THING...
I DON'T KNOW THAT HE CAN HANDLE THE TENSION IN FRONT OF HIS SUPERIORS.

I DON'T KNOW IF HE CAN DO WELL WITH SO LITTLE EVIDENCE...
THERE'S A HIERARCHY PROBLEM, SO THERE'S LITTLE THAT CAN BE DONE.
RIGHT, LITTLE GO-SHIN?
MEOW
HUH...?
I TOLD YOU CHANGE HIS NAME!
WHAT'S WRONG WITH HIS NAME?
UH...
WHAT'S WRONG?

I DRAGGED EVERYONE INTO THIS...
...BUT I FEEL LIKE I CAN'T DO ANYTHING.
DO YOU REALLY THINK YOU DRAGGED THEM?
YOU DIDN'T FORCE ANYONE TO DO ANYTHING. THEY CAME HERE ON THEIR OWN.
YOU DON'T NEED A COLLEGE DEGREE OR TO WEAR A SUIT AND TIE TO KNOW THE VALUE OF YOUR LIFE.
TRUST ME. AND IF THINGS GO WRONG, THEY'LL FIX THEMSELVES.
LOSING ISN'T SCARY.
*허벌나게 조져불자
* LET'S MESS SHIT UP
IT'S JUST SCARY TO BE ALONE WHEN YOU'RE LOSING.
JUST STAND BY HIM.
THAT'S ENOUGH.

THIS FEELS LIKE...
THIS SOUP IS SALTY.
...LIVING IN THE SAME HOUSE AS AN EX YOU CAN'T EVEN STAND TO BE IN THE SAME ROOM WITH.
DIDN'T YOU TELL ME DIABETES RUNS IN YOUR FAMILY?

WHY'D YOU DO IT?
MEETING SOMEONE YOU KILLED WITH YOUR OWN HANDS ON YOUR WAY TO WORK.
SOMETHING YOU CAN'T IMAGINE BEING IN THE PLACE YOU LEAST EXPECT IT.
THE FEELINGS OF CONFUSION AND TERROR CAUSED BY THE UNIMAGINABLE.

WE REWARD
SSES FOR
IEN WE'RE
IPLOYED,
E'RE FAM
HEN WE'R
IRED, WE
IGS TO T
I DON'T BREAK EASILY. COME FIND OUT.
WHEN WE'RE EMPLOYED, WE'RE FAMILY. WHEN WE'RE FIRED, WE'RE PIGS TO THE SLAUGHTER.
ARE WE EXPENDABLE TO YOU?
THERE IS A UNION BY YOUR SIDE
I DON'T BREAK EASILY. COME FIND OUT.
WE REWARD BOSSES FOR FIRING EMPLOYEES
I DIDN'T THINK YOU WOULD COME, BUT HERE YOU ARE.
I HAVE THINGS TO DO AT HOME... BUT I COULDN'T MISS THIS.
STAND OVER HERE.
LOOK AT HIS FACE.
WE'RE BAREL
GETTING
WE'RE FO
TO SMILE.
THER
UNIO
YOUR

PUTAIN!
IT MAY BE GOOD PUBLICITY, BUT WOULDN'T IT BE DANGEROUS? IT WOULD BE GROUNDS FOR DISCIPLINARY ACTION.
MAYBE, MAYBE NOT. THAT'S UP TO A JUDGE.
IF WE PROVOKE THEM FOR NO REASON AND JOON-CHEOL GETS FIRED, EMPLOYEE MORALE WILL PLUMMET.
WHY UNIONIZE IF YOU'RE GOING TO STAY QUIET?
MR. LEE.
FIGHTING IS ABOUT CHECKING BOUNDARIES.
SOME PEOPLE WILL REWARD YOU WITH A TROPHY FOR HITTING THEM, BUT SOME WILL HIT BACK.
YOU DON'T KNOW WHO YOU'RE DEALING WITH UNTIL YOU POKE THEM.

THE COMPANY DIDN'T KNOW WHAT KIND OF PERSON YOU WERE.
WHAT I DO MAKES PEOPLE PUSH BACK AT ME.
I FIGHT TO SEE HOW MUCH THEY'LL BUDGE.
IF YOU DON'T FIGHT, YOU DON'T KNOW WHERE THE BOUNDARIES ARE AND YOU CAN'T CROSS THEM.
THE IMPORTANT THING IS...

...IT MAY BE YOUR FIRST TIME, BUT IT'S THEIR FIRST TIME, TOO.
THEY'RE AS SCARED AS YOU ARE.
WHEN WE'RE EMPLOYED, WE'RE FAMILY.
ARE WE EXPENDABLE TO YOU?
HEY! YOUNG PEOPLE SHOWING SOME COURAGE!

WE
ABLE
U?
IS THIS COMPANY A LABOR OPPRESSOR?!
MAKE YOURSELVES SEEN!
EXCUSE ME.
CAN I GET BY?
THUD
ARE WE
PENDABL
TO YOU?
THERE IS A UNION BY YOUR SIDE
WHEN WE'RE EMPLOYED, WE'RE FAMILY.
WHEN WE'RE FIRED, WE'RE PIGS TO THE SLAUGHTER.
THERE IS A UNION BY YOUR SIDE
WE REWARD
OSSES FOR
NG EMPLOYEES

WE DON'T KNOW THE INTENT OF THE EYES LOOKING AT US.
EXCITEMENT, FEAR, OR RIDICULE?
WHAT IS CLEAR IS THAT WE'RE THE ONLY ONES MOVING IN THIS SILENT, FROZEN SPACE.
EVERYONE IS WATCHING US.

확
RIP
북
RIP
부
욱
RIIP
ARE YOU CRAZY?
HOW COULD YOU STAB ME IN THE BACK LIKE THIS?!
YOUR... WHAT?
"WE REWARD BOSSES FOR FIRING EMPLOYEES"?!
IS THIS ABOUT ME?!

IN FRONT OF ALL THOSE PEOPLE?! REALLY? HOW COULD YOU?!
I HIRED YOU AND TAUGHT YOU HOW TO DO THE JOB, AND THIS IS HOW YOU TREAT ME?
WOW. I'M GOING TO LOSE MY MIND.
TO THINK YOU'D TURN OUT LIKE THIS...
WHY ME?
...WHAT?
YOU'RE THE ONE WHO STABBED ME IN THE BACK.
YOU... WHO TOLD YOU THAT?

THAT'S NOT THE POINT RIGHT NOW, IS IT?!
WHY ME?!
THERE'S MIN-HO AND DAE-JIN... WHY DID YOU STAB ME IN THE BACK?!
YOU... YOU...
YEAH?
WHAT ABOUT ME?

YOU...
I THOUGHT IT WOULD BE EASIEST...
WHAT...?
AH... SHIT...
WHAT THE HELL?
JOON-CHEOL.
EVERYONE'S GOING TO GET FIRED EVENTUALLY.
I THOUGHT YOU'D UNDERSTAND. YOU KNOW HOW IT WORKS.
IF I DON'T CLEAR THINGS OUT, I'LL BE FIRED MYSELF...

JOON-CHEOL!
I'M REALLY SORRY I DIDN'T EXPLAIN THE SITUATION TO YOU.
BUT IT'S NOT FAIR THAT THEY'LL FIRE ALL OF US.
DON'T YOU THINK I SHOULD BE AROUND TO TAKE CARE OF YOU GUYS?
DO YOU THINK MR. LEE THINKS OF YOU AS MUCH AS I DO?
HE'S USING YOU TO GET REVENGE ON HIS BOSS!
DON'T LOOK AT ME LIKE THAT!
I'M A SCUMBAG, BUT NOT THE SCUMBAG THAT YOU THINK I AM!
I DIDN'T CREATE THIS SITUATION! YOU DID!
I WAS HOPING YOU WOULD JUST LEAVE QUIETLY AND RECOGNIZE YOUR PLACE...
WHY DID YOU MAKE THINGS SO HARD?!

JOON-CHEOL, IT'S NOT TOO LATE.
WHEN YOU GO TO THE DISCIPLINARY COMMITTEE, ADMIT YOU'VE DONE WRONG AND BEG FOR MERCY. THEN I'LL TRY TO SAVE YOU.
IF YOU GO WITH MR. LEE, YOU'LL ONLY BE HURTING YOURSELF.
YOU KNOW I THINK OF YOU LIKE A BROTHER, RIGHT?
HUH? JOON-CHEOL! LISTEN TO ME!
THE FIRST THING YOU NEED TO ESCAPE FROM AN ISLAND...

...IS THE EXISTENCE OF ANOTHER ISLAND.
JOON-CHEOL, I LIKE YOU A LOT.
YOU'RE A GOOD GUY, AND YOU ACCEPT ME FOR WHO I AM.
BUT...
...IF YOU MENTION THAT BASTARD IN FRONT OF ME EVER AGAIN...
...IT'S REALLY OVER.
HEY, JOON-CHEOL, DO YOU HEAR ME?
HUH?

HEY, KYEONG-SIK.
WHO TREATS THEIR LITTLE BROTHER LIKE THIS?
WERE YOU BEATEN AT HOME?
IF POSSIBLE...
...A BETTER ISLAND.

THERE IS A
UNION BY
YOUR SIDE
HUH?
AH, HELLO, MISS SONG.
THERE IS A
UNION BY
YOUR SIDE
ISN'T THIS AGAINST THE LAW?
AH... THERE'S CASE LAW THAT SAYS UNION ACTIVITIES DURING BREAKS ARE PERMITTED AS LONG AS IT DOESN'T INFRINGE ON THE RIGHTS OF OTHER WORKERS.
THE COMPANY MIGHT TRY TO SUE ME FOR OBSTRUCTION OF BUSINESS, BUT WE'LL SEE...
HO HO HO HO.
?
SO YOU'RE AN EXPERT NOW?
I HAD A FEELING IT WOULD GO LIKE THIS SOONER OR LATER.
WHAT?
THERE IS A

DON'T YOU REMEMBER THE FIRST TIME WE MET?
IF EVERYTHING'S OPERATIONAL UNTIL CLOSING TIME, WHEN WILL WE ACTUALLY GO HOME?
THAT'S THE BEST WAY TO DO IT. EVERYBODY KNOWS THAT.
IT'S JUST THAT NO ONE WANTS TO DO IT.
DO YOU KNOW HOW MANY EMPLOYEES ARE LEFT AT CLOSING? TWO.
TWO PEOPLE WILL HAVE TO CLEAN EVERYTHING UP AND PUT EVERYTHING BACK THEMSELVES.
BEFORE YOU TELL US HOW THINGS SHOULD GO, YOU SHOULD ACTUALLY VISIT THE STORE.
YOU DON'T KNOW HOW TO DO ANYTHING BUT SIT BEHIND YOUR DESK AND TALK NONSENSE, CAUSING TROUBLE FOR THE REST OF US.

벌
SCRAPE
떡
ISN'T THAT A BIT MUCH?
DID I SAY SOMETHING THAT ISN'T TRUE, MR. LEE?
IT MAY BE TRUE, BUT THAT DOESN'T MEAN YOU CAN TREAT YOUR INSTRUCTOR SO POORLY.
SORRY.
OUR PEOPLE CAN BE A BIT ROUGH AROUND THE EDGES...

NO. IN FACT, I'VE HEARD THE SAME THING AT EVERY STORE I'VE GONE TO FOR TRAINING.
I KNOW.
I KNOW WHAT I SAID ISN'T REALISTIC...
...BUT...I GET THE FEELING IT ISN'T ONLY ABOUT THE TRAINING MATERIAL.
YOU'RE RIGHT.
NO ONE DOES THAT WHEN THERE'S A MALE INSTRUCTOR.
THAT'S WHY I WAS SO ANGRY.
THAT'S WHEN I STARTED TO THINK YOU WERE A BIT OF A PECULIAR GUY.
AH, NOW I REMEMBER.
THINGS HAVE BEEN TOUGH LATELY?
WELL... CERTAINLY NOT EASY.
THERE IS A UNION BY YOUR SIDE
KEEP GOING. SAVE ME SOME TROUBLE.

WHAT?
GASTON'S BEEN DRIVING ME CRAZY ABOUT REDUCING STAFF.
NOW HE'S TARGETING YOU, SO KEEP FIGHTING.
I HAVEN'T QUIT MY JOB YET THANKS TO YOU.
ONCE AGAIN, YOU'VE MADE THINGS A BIT EASIER FOR ME.
DOES THAT SOUND SELFISH?
THERE IS A
HERE COMES THE BOSS. I BETTER NOT BE SEEN WITH THE OUTCAST.
THERE IS A
UNION BY
YOUR SIDE
STAY STRONG, MR. LEE.
THANKS.

WHAT THE HELL ARE YOU DOING DURING WORK HOURS?
RETURN TO WORK IMMEDIATELY!
"MANAGERS MANAGE THEIR OWN WORK."
"THAT'S HOW IT WORKS AT FOURMIS."
YOU'VE ALWAYS EMPHASIZED THAT.
THERE IS A UNION BY

MANAGERS DON'T HAVE SET WORK HOURS OR PREDESIGNATED BREAKS.
THE RULE THAT MEANT WE COULDN'T AVOID WORKING LATE IS NOW MY WEAPON.
WHO IS THIS?
ARE YOU PART OF THE DISCIPLINARY COMMITTEE?
THEY'RE PART OF THE HUMAN RESOURCES DEPARTMENT AT HEADQUARTERS.
THEN I'LL JOIN YOU AS AN OBSERVER.
IS THERE A LABOR UNION OBSERVER PROVISION IN THE DISCIPLINARY COMMITTEE RULES?
I DIDN'T SEE IT.
SO IS THERE A THIRD-PARTY OBSERVER PROVISION?
IF I CAN'T GO IN, NEITHER CAN THEY!

FINE. COME ON, THEN, IF YOU'RE ABLE.
MR. LEE, I'LL BE FINE.
WE PREPARED WELL.

철컥
CLACK

HEY, JOON-CHEOL HWANG.
WHO TOLD YOU TO SIT DOWN?
ISN'T THAT THE ATTITUDE THAT GOT YOU HERE?
STAND UP!

YOU... YOU SHOULDN'T SPEAK SO INFORMALLY.
WHY? DOES THE EMPLOYEE HANDBOOK SAY HOW I SHOULD ADDRESS YOU DURING A DISCIPLINARY HEARING?
I KNOW HOW MUCH YOU LOVE THAT HANDBOOK.
SIT DOWN, MR. HWANG.
WHAT ARE YOU DOING? SIT DOWN.

...
WE DECLARE THE SESSION OPEN.
DIRECTOR OF HUMAN RESOURCES, PLEASE PROCEED.
THE SUBJECT TO DISCIPLINARY ACTION IS JOON-CHEOL HWANG, EMPLOYEE NUMBER 98000XXX.
IS THAT CORRECT?
THAT'S CORRECT.

...?
HUH?
CASE OVERVIEW.
AH! CASE OVERVIEW.
LET ME DESCRIBE THE CIRCUMSTANCES OF WHAT HAPPENED.

ON WEDNESDAY, MAY 28, 2003, AT APPROXIMATELY 8:00 P.M., FOURMIS EMPLOYEE JOON-CHEOL HWANG...
...WAS WITH YEONGGWANG FISHERIES' CEO AND EMPLOYEES.
...300,000 WON WORTH OF ENTERTAINMENT...
HE RECEIVED MONEY FROM CEO BOK-SEONG KIM.
THAT IS ALL.
THE DISCIPLINARY COMMITTEE HAS BEEN CONVENED FOR THE ABOVE REASONS. YOU MAY ASK QUESTIONS TO THE PERSON BEING DISCIPLINED.
NEXT, WE WILL HEAR THE STATEMENT OF THE PERSON BEING DISCIPLINED.

MR. HWANG...
...DO YOU AGREE WITH THE DESCRIPTION OF WHAT HAPPENED?
YES, I DO. HOWEVER, MR. HEO WAS ALSO PRESENT.
AND HE TOLD ME TO ACCEPT THE MONEY SO THAT I COULD TAKE A TAXI HOME.
HERE'S A STATEMENT FROM SOMEONE ELSE WHO WAS WITH US AT THE KARAOKE PLACE.
MR. HEO, IS THIS TRUE?
NO, I THINK MR. HWANG IS GIVING FALSE TESTIMONY.
ALSO, YEONGGWANG'S MANAGER MR. MIN-SEOK CHOI AND I LOOK VERY SIMILAR PHYSICALLY...
...SO THAT MAY HAVE CAUSED SOME MISUNDERSTANDING AND CONFUSION.
AT THE TIME, I WAS IN A MEETING WITH ONE OF OUR DRIED FISH SUPPLIERS. YOU CAN CHECK WITH THEM, IF YOU'D LIKE.

KYEONG-SIK...
MR. HWANG IS KNOWN FOR HIS OVERINDULGING AND HIS REQUESTS FOR MONEY.
EMPLOYEES OF YEONGGWANG FISHERIES RESENTED HIM...
...BUT HE THREATENED SEVERING BUSINESS IF HIS DEMANDS WEREN'T MET.
THAT IS WHAT THEIR CEO, BOK-SEONG KIM, HAS TESTIFIED.

HEY, HWANG! ARE YOU STILL WAITING FOR A PROMOTION?
COME WORK FOR ME! I'LL GIVE YOU A RAISE!
THAT IS ALSO WHAT MR. MIN-SEOK CHOI HAS TESTIFIED...
PLEASE TREAT OUR CONTRACTED WORKERS WELL.
YOU'RE THE ONLY ONE AT FOURMIS I TRUST.
THE FACT THAT JOON-CHEOL HWANG WAS THE ONLY ONE PRESENT WAS CONFIRMED BY...
...CONTRACTED WORKER SEONG-MIN JEONG...
HEY, JOON-CHEOL, THERE'S GOING TO BE A PERMANENT POSITION AVAILABLE SOON, RIGHT?
MENTION MY NAME. WE CAN HELP EACH OTHER OUT.
...AND CONTRACTED WORKER JIN-HYEOK BYEON, WHO HAS ALREADY PROVIDED TESTIMONY.

MR. HWANG.
THERE'S A NUMBER OF STATEMENTS THAT CORROBORATE EACH OTHER.
ARE YOU SAYING THAT ALL OF THESE WITNESSES ARE LYING?
THIS... THIS...
...THIS IS ABOUT MR. HEO.
HE HAS REPEATEDLY RECEIVED MONEY FROM SEONG-PIL.
I HAVE WRITTEN TESTIMONY FROM SEONG-PIL RIGHT HERE.

THAT WASN'T ME...
ALL OF THOSE PEOPLE...
...SEONG-MIN AND JIN-HYEOK... AREN'T THOSE KINDS OF PEOPLE...
IF THERE ARE NO FURTHER QUESTIONS, WE CAN...
JIN-HYEOK... REALLY...
JIN-HYEOK...!
콰
당
CLANG
JIN-HYEOK BYEON!
YOU MENTIONED EARLIER THAT THERE IS TESTIMONY FROM JIN-HYEOK BYEON, RIGHT?

YOU SAID THAT JIN-HYEOK TESTIFIED HE WAS WITH ME AT THE TIME!
YES... SO?
JOON-CHEOL HWANG! HAVE YOU GONE CRAZY?!
SIT DOWN!
JOON-CHEOL HWANG!
WAIT A MINUTE... WAIT A MINUTE...
WHERE IS IT? I DIDN'T DELETE IT...
JIN-HYEOK BYEON... JIN-HYEOK BYEON...
THERE IT IS!
THERE IT IS!

JIN-HYEOK BYEON WAS ON VACATION AT THE TIME!
Jin-hyuk Byeon
Hey Joon-Cheol! Are you working hard covering for me? Have fun without me! Hahaha!
HERE'S A TEXT THAT PROVES HE WAS TRAVELING!
HOW COULD SOMEONE WHO WASN'T IN TOWN BE HAVING DRINKS WITH ME AT KARAOKE?!
THIS IS ALL MANIPULATION!
...
HOW CAN YOU SAY MY STATEMENTS ARE FALSE AFTER YOU SET ALL OF THIS UP?!
I SAID SIT DOWN!
IT'S THE TRUTH!

LET GO OF ME!
CAN THE HR MANAGER CONFIRM?
UH... WE DON'T HANDLE CONTRACT WORKERS' VACATIONS...
THE HEAD OF THE DEPARTMENT TAKES CARE OF THOSE SCHEDULES!
MR. HEO HAS THE SCHEDULES!
GET THEM NOW!
RIGHT NOW!
QUICKLY!
STOP LYING!

WHAT... WHAT ARE YOU TALKING ABOUT?
IF YOU THINK IT'S FOR THE BEST, GO AHEAD.
YES. YES, SIR.
...
...

FUCK THIS!!
MERDE!

EXCUSE ME.
MR. HWANG.
BOSS...
GREAT WORK.
THAT WAS EXCELLENT.

COFFEE & RESTAURANT
YOU HAVEN'T CHANGED AT ALL.
HOW CAN YOU ASK ME TO PROVIDE A DEPOSITION?

DISCIPLINARY COMMITTEE RESULTS: REPRIMAND.
WE WON.
NOTHING CHANGED, BUT EVERYTHING CHANGED.
THE FRIGHTENED EYES PEEKING OUT OF LINE TO COUNT HOW MANY PEOPLE WERE AROUND...
...STARTED LOOKING AHEAD, RATHER THAN TO THE SIDE.

To: Go-shin Gu
Director, we won!
HOW ARE THE KIDS?
...MIN-JOON MUST BE IN MIDDLE SCHOOL.
THANKS TO YOU.
YOU KNOW THAT... I HATE YOU, RIGHT?

I DON'T EVEN WANT TO TAKE YOUR MONEY.
I ONLY ACCEPT IT FOR THE KIDS.
RIIIIIING
RIIIIIING
?
HAS CHEOL-SEUNG...
...REACHED OUT TO YOU?

단결 투쟁

* BACK TO THE FACTORY!

경 찰
POLICE

I DON'T KNOW. THERE'S TALK OF A JOB SOMEWHERE...
...BUT WHO WOULD WANT TO HIRE HIM AT THIS POINT?
I REALLY...
...HATE YOU.

I STAYED UP ALL NIGHT...
...TRYING TO REMIND HIM THAT HE'S A FATHER.
BUT EVERY TIME OUR EYES MET...
...HE LOOKED LIKE A CHILD ABOUT TO GO ON A TRIP.
SAYING THAT HE COULD WIN...
...THAT HE WOULD PROTECT EVERYONE.

HUFF
HUFF
HUFF

CHEOL-SEUNG... LIE DOWN... YOU'RE BADLY HURT.
YOU NEED TO LIE DOWN.
HONEY, PLEASE...

PEOPLE ARE QUIETLY SWEPT AWAY LIKE SANDCASTLES IF LEFT ALONE...

WHY... WHY DID YOU BRING THEM TOGETHER...
...SO THAT THEY COULD BE DESTROYED?

KILL ME...

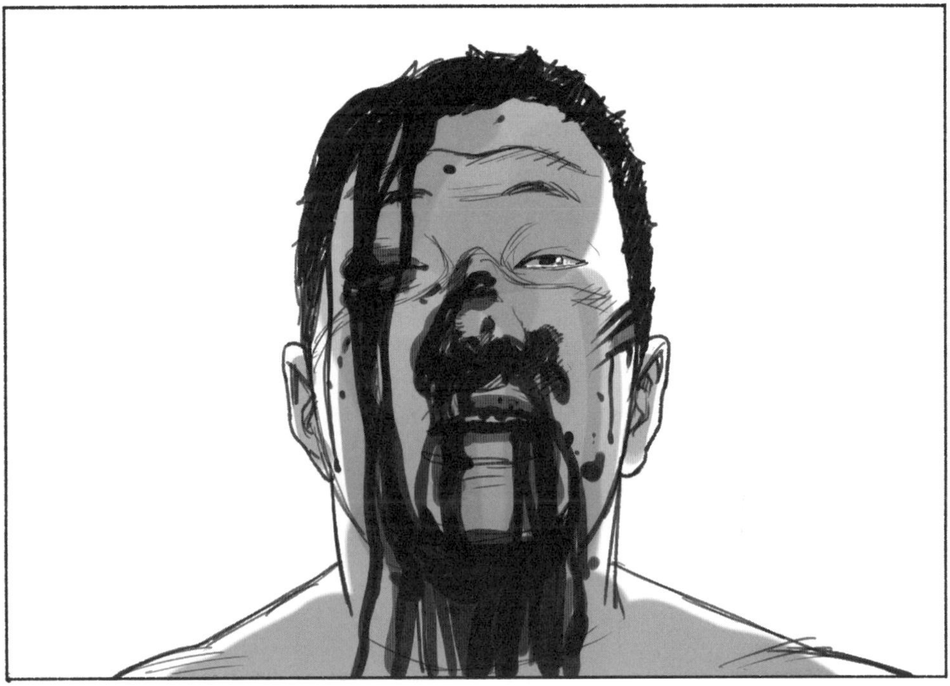

I'M SURE ONE OF THEM WILL BREAK THROUGH.

3
1
B1
B2
WHAT...
...AHH...
...WHAT ARE YOU BASTARDS GOING TO DO?
YOU'LL HAVE TO KILL ME...

KILL ME!!

THE ONE AT THE FOREFRONT, THE SHARPEST OF THEM ALL...
...IS THE ONE WHO BREAKS THROUGH FIRST.

MR. GU!
WE WON...
THE ONE WHO PIERCES LIKE AN AWL.

THE ENROLLMENT RATE IS LESS THAN 20%.
NO, IF WE TRY TOO EARLY, IT WILL FAIL.
HUH? WHAT DID THE COMPANY DO, TURN A BLIND EYE?
M... MR. GU...
...

ARE YOU SURPRISED, SOO-IN? I HAVE TO DO THIS FOUR TIMES A DAY.
CHRONIC RENAL FAILURE.
UH... SINCE WHEN...
SINCE I WAS TORTURED.
WHEN THE MILITARY REGIME WAS STILL IN POWER.

DON'T LOOK AT ME WITH ADMIRATION IN YOUR EYES.
I'M NOT THE PERSON YOU IMAGINE I AM.

Chapter 3

WHEN DID YOU GO TO NORTH KOREA?
...WHAT?
YOU WENT TO NORTH KOREA. TELL US WHEN.
...
MR. KIM, I DON'T THINK HE REMEMBERS.
LET'S HELP HIM.

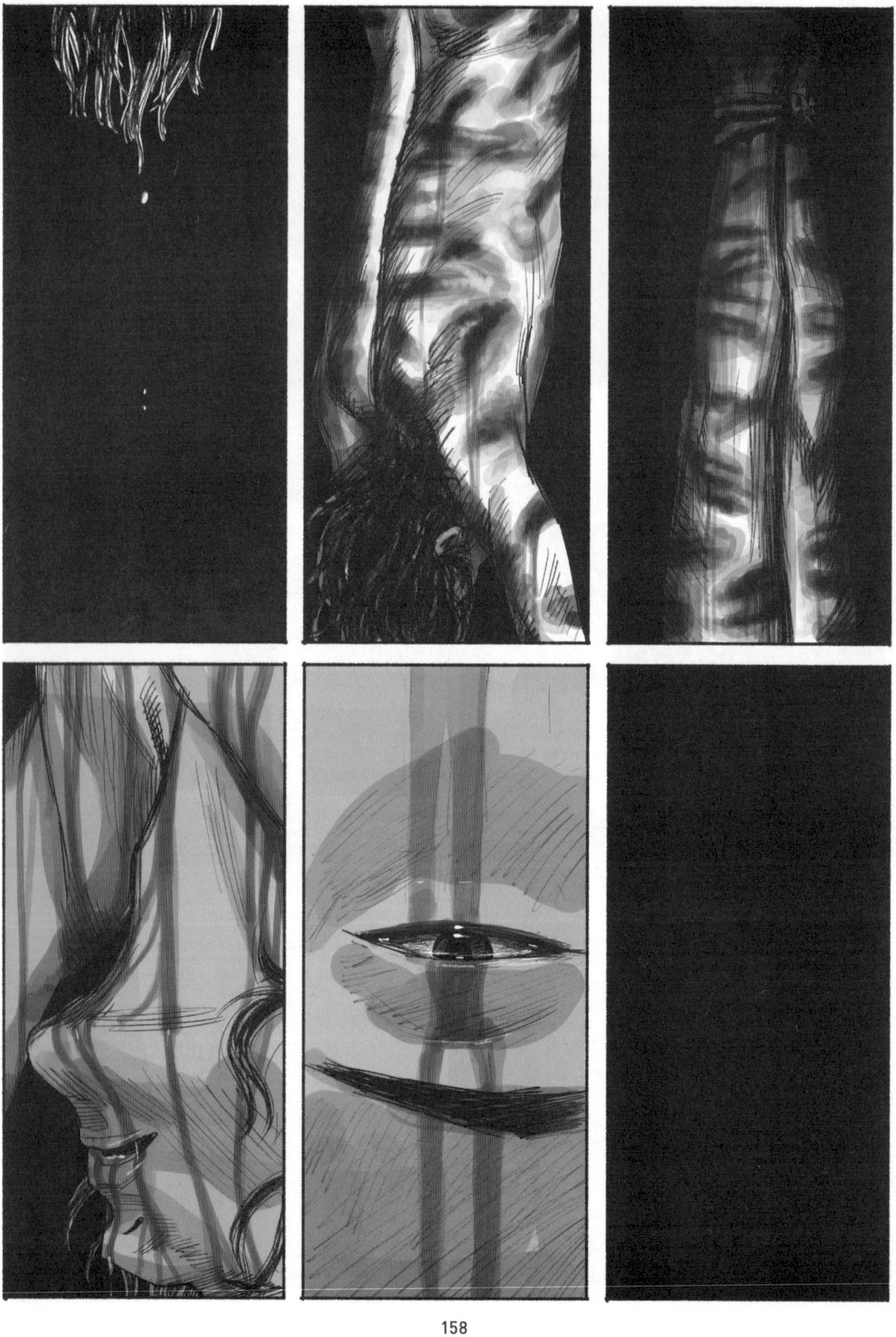

WHY DO WE ALWAYS EAT THERE? THE FOOD ISN'T GOOD. LET'S GET SOMETHING ELSE.
THE GIRL WHO WORKS THERE IS CUTE.
BUT SHE'S PRETTY OLD!
I'M NOT A KID EITHER! AND STILL SINGLE! CAN'T I BE SHAMELESS?

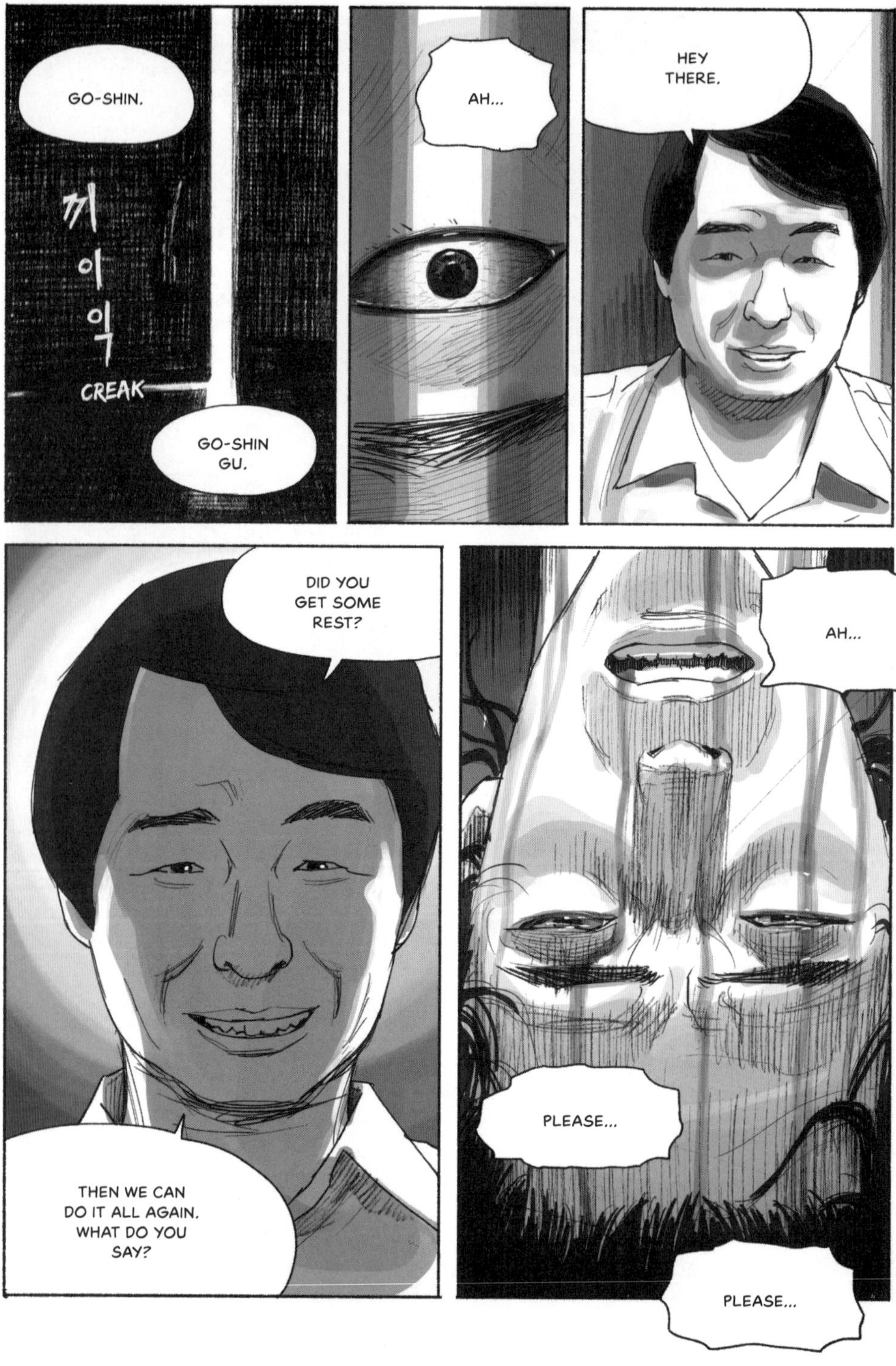
GO-SHIN.
끼이익
CREAK
GO-SHIN GU.
AH...
HEY THERE.
DID YOU GET SOME REST?
THEN WE CAN DO IT ALL AGAIN. WHAT DO YOU SAY?
AH...
PLEASE...
PLEASE...

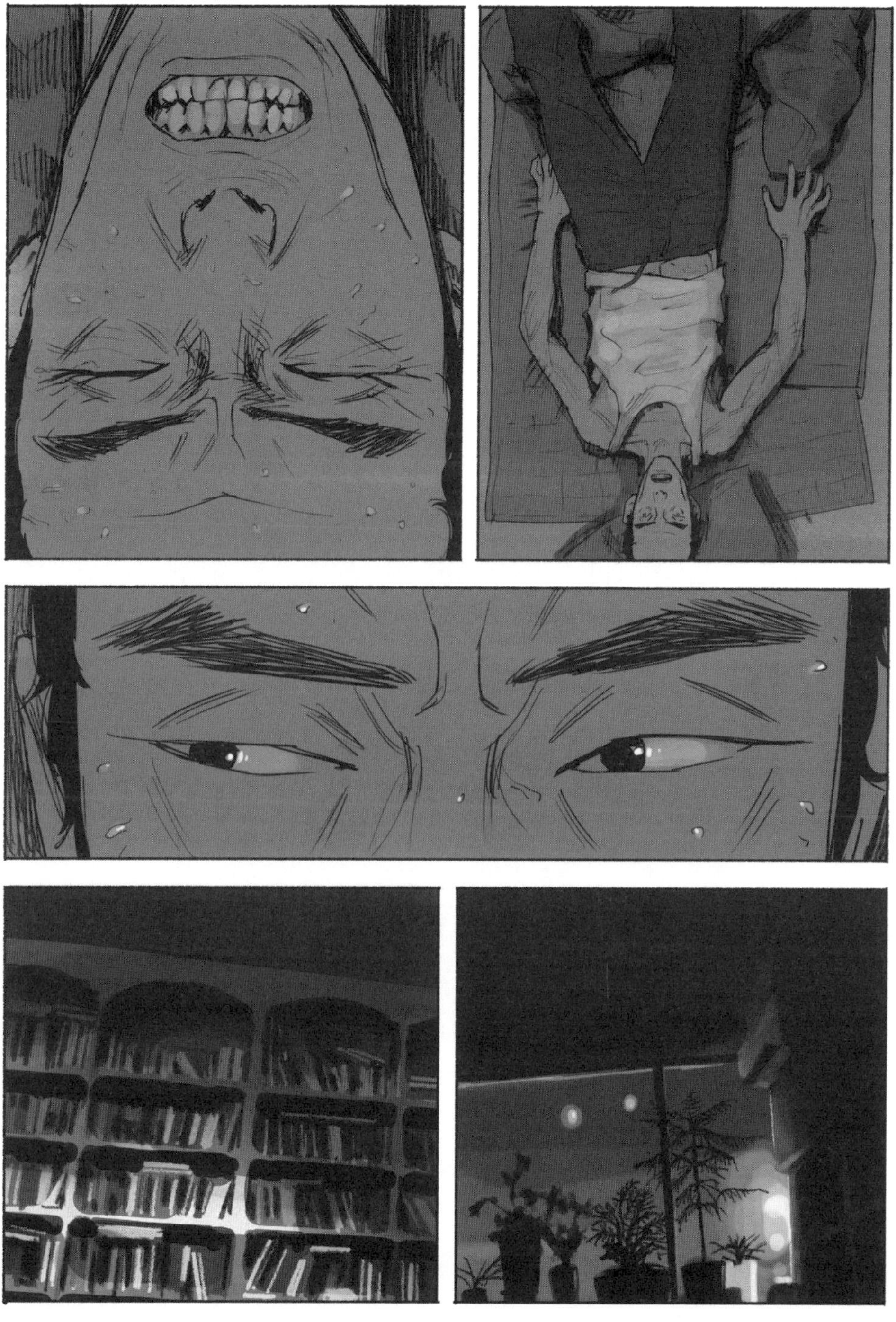

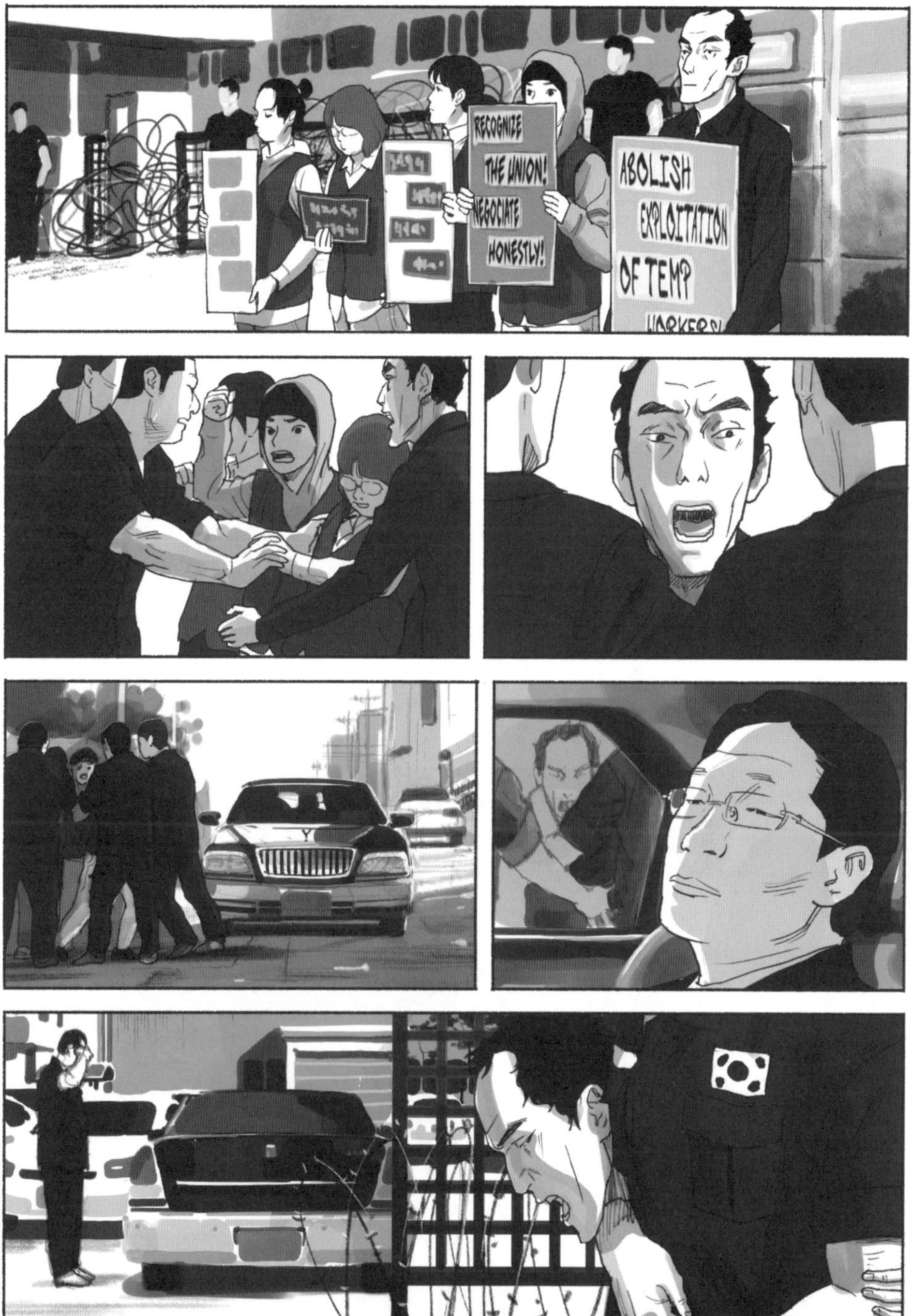
RECOGNIZE THE UNION! NEGOCIATE HONESTLY!
ABOLISH EXPLOITATION OF TEMP

* UNIVERSITY STUDENT CENTER

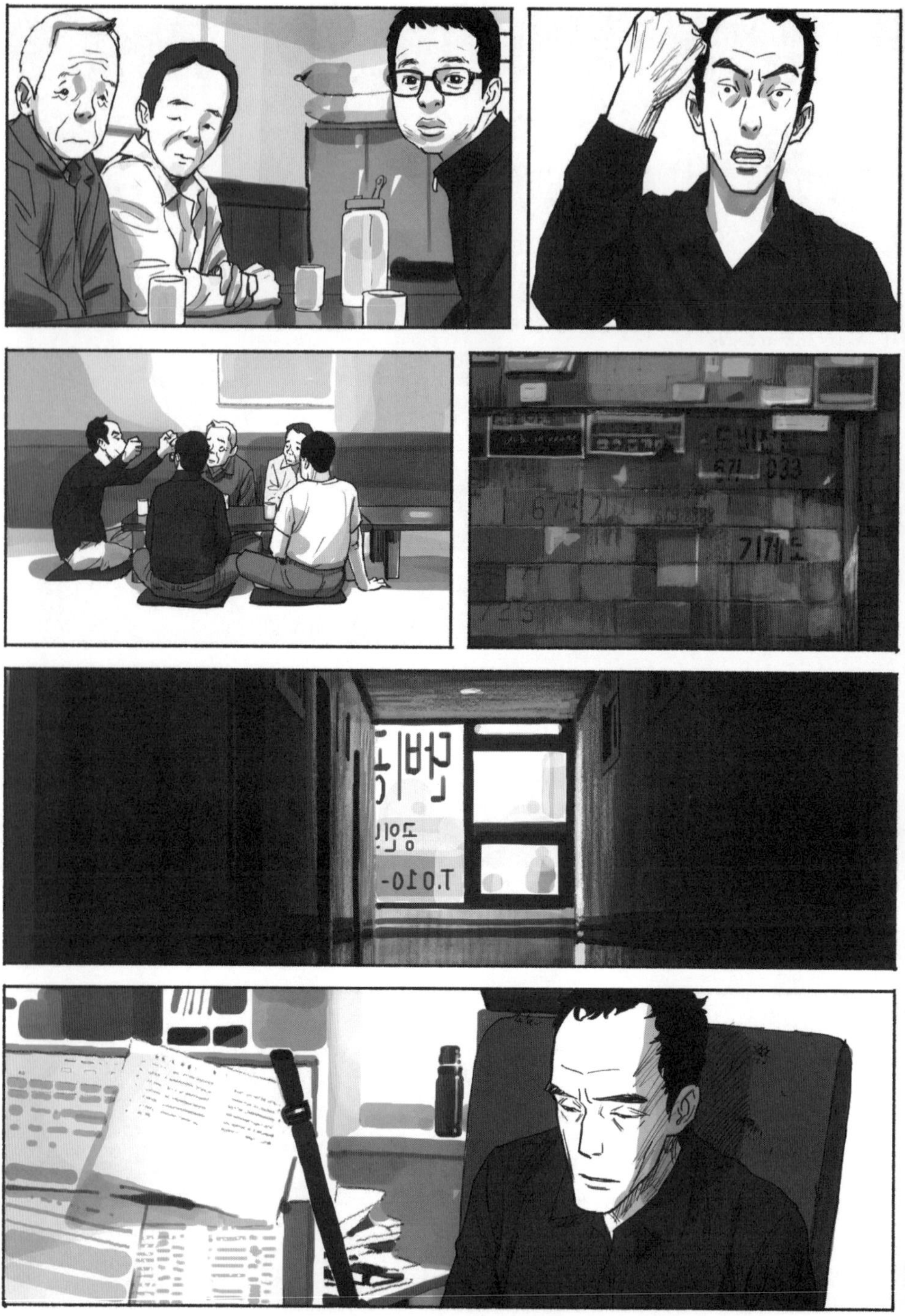

BZZZZZ
우우우웅
우우웅
BZZZZZ
Fourmis Soo-in Lee
HELLO, SOO-IN.
MR. GU, YOU DON'T SOUND GOOD. ARE YOU OKAY?
DID YOU CALL JUST TO HEAR MY VOICE? WHAT IS IT?
I WAS JUST CALLING TO CHECK IF YOU WERE GOING TO MAKE IT TO THE MEETING TODAY.
IF YOU DON'T FEEL WELL, WE CAN RESCHEDULE.
I'LL BE THERE.
...
WE CAN DO IT ANOTHER DAY.
I SAID I'LL BE THERE!

YOU'RE COMMITTING UNFAIR LABOR PRACTICES!
PLEASE DON'T INTERFERE WITH OUR MEETING!
UNION ACTIVITY IS PROTECTED BY THE LAW!

OH! MR. GU!
EVERYONE, YOUR INSTRUCTOR IS HERE.
AHH...

ALRIGHT, THEN...
...LET'S GET TO WORK!

WHEN WE'RE EMPLOYED, WE'RE FAMILY.
WHEN WE'RE FIRED, WE'RE PIGS TO THE SLAUGHTER.
ARE WE EXPENDABLE TO YOU?
THERE IS A UNION BY YOUR SIDE
I DON'T BREAK EASILY.
COME FIND OUT.
WE REWARD BOSSES FOR FIRING EMPLOYEES

MR. LEE.
LET IT GO.
LET THEM LISTEN. MAYBE THEY'LL LEARN SOMETHING.

YOU STAND HERE.
AND YOU, OVER HERE.
THAT'S MUCH BETTER. YOU LOOK IMPORTANT.
OKAY, THEN!
LET THE LESSONS BEGIN!

DO YOU REMEMBER THE IMF BAILOUT IN 1997?
WHEN ALL THE WORKERS GOT FIRED...
...AND THE BUSINESSMEN RAN AWAY FROM THEIR CREDITORS?
THEN HOUSEWIVES POURED INTO FACTORIES, RESTAURANTS, AND GROCERY STORES LOOKING FOR WORK?
THAT'S NOT THE CASE HERE. OUR KIDS ARE GROWN, SO WE WORK TO HAVE SOMETHING TO DO.
TO EARN POCKET MONEY.
AH! POCKET MONEY?
AND YOU GOT UP BEFORE DAWN, AND MISSED SEEING YOUR KIDS BEFORE SCHOOL, TO EARN POCKET MONEY?

...YOU TAKE PAINKILLERS FOR YOUR HIPS, SHOULDERS, KNEES, AND ARMS...
...YOU DON'T HAVE TIME TO USE THE BATHROOM, SO YOU RISK INFECTIONS...
...YOU'RE ON YOUR FEET ALL DAY AND YOUR LEGS ARE SWOLLEN...
...YOU DON'T HAVE THE STRENGTH TO CLEAN THE HOUSE WHEN YOUR MOTHER-IN-LAW IS COMING OVER...
"HELLO. THANK YOU. YOU'RE WELCOME." OVER AND OVER TO CUSTOMERS.
TO EARN POCKET MONEY.
IT'S NOT JUST POCKET MONEY. IT'S MONEY YOU'VE EARNED KILLING YOURSELVES AT WORK.
IT'S COMPENSATION YOU'VE EARNED FOR DOING WORK FOR SOMEONE ELSE. AND WORKING PEOPLE HAVE WORKING PEOPLE'S RIGHTS!

BUT LET'S SAY YOU *ARE* JUST WORKING FOR POCKET MONEY.
I'M SURE THERE ARE PEOPLE WHO HAVE MORE THAN ENOUGH MONEY BUT CAN'T STAND THE IDEA OF NOT WORKING.
SO WHY ARE YOU HERE?
YOU WERE SCARED TO JOIN THE UNION.
"I'M SCARED TO DEATH, SO WHY AM I LISTENING TO SOME OLD MAN TALK ABOUT WORKERS' RIGHTS?"
IS IT BECAUSE THESE TWO HANDSOME MANAGERS PERSUADED YOU?
EVEN IF NO ONE HAS TOLD YOU, YOU ALREADY KNOW IT.
WHETHER YOU'RE HERE TO EARN POCKET MONEY OR NEED TO MAKE ENDS MEET...
...WORKERS DON'T DESERVE TO BE TREATED THIS WAY!

WOULD YOU LIKE IT IF YOUR KIDS SAW YOU AT WORK?
WOULD YOU LET THEM WORK HERE? NO?
WHY NOT? BECAUSE IT'S HARD WORK?
BECAUSE YOU'RE UNDERPAID?
NO?
BECAUSE YOUR MANAGERS, WHO ARE YOUNGER THAN YOU, INSULT YOU...
...SPIT IN YOUR FACE....
...BUT YOU HAVE TO SMILE ALL DAY, WITH YOUR LIPS QUIVERING AND YOUR MOUTH SHUT TIGHT, JUST LIKE THIS.
IT'S EMBARRASSING, AND YOU'RE ASHAMED!
WHY SHOULD PEOPLE WHO DO HONEST WORK BE ASHAMED?
YOU SIGNED A WORK CONTRACT, NOT A SLAVERY CONTRACT!

YOU CAN PRETEND THAT EVERYTHING IS FINE, BUT I KNOW THERE ARE SOME OF YOU WHO LIVE ALONE...
...WHO LIVE FAR FROM YOUR CHILDREN.
IF YOU DIDN'T WORK HERE, YOU WOULDN'T BE ABLE TO PAY YOUR BILLS OR FEED YOUR KIDS.
AND ON TOP OF THAT, YOU GET SICK.
BEING SICK IS ONE THING, BUT YOU STILL HAVE TO GO TO WORK. AND THEN YOUR KIDS GET SICK.
WE LIVE IN A DEVELOPED COUNTRY. IT HAS THE 10TH LARGEST ECONOMY IN THE WORLD!
AND, YET, OUR LIVES ARE MISERABLE!

WE'RE THE ONES WHO SHED BLOOD.
THIS COUNTRY RUNS ON BLEEDING FATHERS...
...DESPERATE MOTHERS...
...CRYING BABIES!
AND WHAT DO THEY TELL US?
THAT WE'RE STILL NOT GIVING ENOUGH!
DO YOU THINK YOUR JOB IS SAFE?
THE COMPANY WANTS TO SAVE A FEW DOLLARS...
...AND REPLACE YOU WITH TEMP WORKERS!
THEY'LL EVEN TRY TO GET YOU TO RETURN TO YOUR POSITION FOR LESS!

YOU CAN'T JUST ACCEPT THAT THIS IS HOW THE ECONOMY WORKS.
THAT YOU'RE HAVING A HARD TIME BECAUSE AREN'T TIGHTENING YOUR BELTS ENOUGH.
IF I TIGHTEN MY BELT ANYMORE, I'LL STARVE TO DEATH ON MY FEET BECAUSE I CAN'T AFFORD A CAR TO GET TO WORK.
THEY'LL ALWAYS TELL YOU THAT IT'S YOUR FAULT.
HOW CAN HUMANS BE SO CRUEL TO OTHER HUMANS?
BECAUSE THEY DON'T THINK OF US AS HUMAN.
TO THEM, WE'RE JUST NUMBERS ON A PIECE OF PAPER.
WE'RE LIVESTOCK THAT THEY CAN BUY AND SELL.
BECAUSE WE DON'T GET ANGRY. WE DON'T FIGHT BACK.

THEY DON'T FEAR US!
RESPECT FOR HUMAN BEINGS COMES FROM FEAR!

A HUMAN BEING GETS ANGRY WHEN SOMETHING IS TAKEN FROM THEM...
...AND IF THEY GET HIT, THEY FIGHT BACK!

GREAT JOB!
GOODBYE, MA'AM.
FEEL LIKE YOU HAVE A LOT OF WEIGHT ON YOUR SHOULDERS?
DO YOU UNDERSTAND WHAT THAT WEIGHT MEANS?

THAT LADY... IS NOT A MEMBER OF THE UNION.
HUH?!
SHE'S A CONTRACT WORKER IN THE FISH DEPARTMENT.
WHAT?! SHE'S NOT A MEMBER OF THE UNION, AND YOU BROUGHT HER HERE?!
I THOUGHT JOON-CHEOL BROUGHT HER.
THIS IS A BIG PROBLEM!
ACCORDING TO FOURMIS REGULATIONS, CONTRACTORS ARE ALLOWED TO JOIN THE UNION.
EVEN IF SHE DID...
...DO YOU THINK YOU CAN PROTECT HER?
THEY'LL FIRE HER AS SOON AS HER CONTRACT ENDS!
MR. JU...
...HOW LONG HAS SHE BEEN WITH THE COMPANY?
UMM...
ABOUT THREE YEARS?

THEN THEY'VE RENEWED HER CONTRACT AT LEAST FOUR TIMES. SHOULDN'T THAT SECURE HER A POSITION BY NOW?
WASN'T THERE A SUPREME COURT CASE THAT SAID IF YOUR CONTRACT IS REPEATEDLY RENEWED OVER A LONG PERIOD OF TIME, YOU'RE GUARANTEED EMPLOYMENT?
WOW, THE SUPREME COURT! THAT'S CASE LAW...
YOU'VE BEEN STUDYING.
YOU'RE RIGHT, BUT IT TAKES FIVE YEARS TO GET A RULING.
DO YOU THINK YOU CAN FIGHT ALONGSIDE HER FOR FIVE YEARS?
SO WE ONLY ACCEPT FULL-TIME EMPLOYEES?!
WHAT KIND OF UNION MAKES DISTINCTIONS BETWEEN EMPLOYEES LIKE THAT?
MR. LEE...
LET'S NOT BE TOO GREAT.

WON HOTEL
WHEN IT COMES TO MANAGERS...
...THEY MUST BE EXCLUDED FROM ELIGIBILITY.
THE UNION DECIDES WHO CAN OR CANNOT JOIN!
HOW CAN THE COMPANY MAKE THAT TYPE OF DECISION?
DO YOU WANT TO END NEGOTIATIONS HERE?

YOU CAN YELL AT ME ALL YOU WANT.
IF IT TAKES A YEAR OR TWO, THE COMPANY DOESN'T CARE.
I'M ONLY SITTING HERE BECAUSE THE DEPARTMENT OF LABOR REQUIRES IT.
YOU BOTH KNOW THERE'S NO REASON FOR THE COMPANY TO PLAY NICE ANYMORE.
THERE ARE ALREADY MANAGERS WHO ARE PART OF THE UNION. ARE YOU SAYING WE HAVE TO KICK THEM OUT?
WHAT UNION CANCELS MEMBERSHIPS?
CONSIDER THE UNION'S POSITION.
WE HAVE...
HERE'S THE AMENDED AGREEMENT.

5. Strike participants will not be penaliz way for pa in the strike.
6. Regarding the scope of membership o nion, the conte he collective bargaining a absolutely complied with, and only three of the managers, team leaders, and non-regular empl members before the conclusion of the collective bargaining agreement (Soo-in Lee, Song-che non-regular members (Yeong-sook Jin, Yeong-ran Bae) are recognized as members. Soo-in L department manager of the Ildong store, cannot become a union chairman in the future.
7. The company and the union will work to restore the company's reputation and support legi union activies.
THIS IS TOO MUCH!
IT'S NOT RIGHT!
SLAM
THE UNION PRESIDENT IS ELECTED BY ITS MEMBERS!
DO YOU REALLY THINK THAT THIS WILL BECOME LEGALLY BINDING?
I DON'T CARE HOW INSIGNIFICANT YOU MAY THINK THIS UNION IS, AREN'T YOU ASHAMED OF YOURSELF FOR PROPOSING THIS?!

FINE! WE'RE DONE NEGOTIATING!
I'LL GO AS FAR AS I CAN BY MYSELF, EVEN IF IT MEANS HANGING MYSELF IN FRONT OF THE MAIN STORE IN THE END!
LET'S SEE WHO WINS!
THE COMPANY KNOWS HOW FAR I AM WILLING TO GO.

I WAS SHOCKED. I HAD NO INTEREST IN NEGOTIATING AFTER THAT.
ONCE MR. LEE'S NAME CAME UP...
WOW... EVEN THE HEAD OFFICE KNOWS WHAT YOU'RE MADE OF.
A REAL TOUGH GUY!
ISN'T IT A BIT UNFAIR TO DETERMINE WHO IS ELIGIBLE TO JOIN THE UNION DURING NEGOTIATIONS?
UNFAIR, YES. BUT STILL LEGAL.
WHAT ABOUT CONTRACTORS? IS CONTRACT WORK A BARGAINING ISSUE?
YES... WE'RE STILL DISCUSSING THAT, TOO.
SO YOU'RE SAYING THEY COULD BAN THEM?
OVER 30% OF OUR WORKERS ARE CONTRACTORS, AND WE'RE GOING TO ABANDON THEM?

MR. LEE, THAT'S A BIT HARSH ISN'T IT?
NO ONE'S ABANDONING ANYONE. IT'S NOT ABOUT WHAT WE WANT, IT'S ABOUT WE CAN DO.
IF WE EXCLUDE MANAGERS, WE MIGHT BE ABLE TO KEEP CONTRACT WORKERS. IS THAT THE WAY WE SHOULD GO?
SHOULD WE CANCEL YOUR MEMBERSHIP, MR. LEE?
I DON'T THINK THAT'S APPROPRIATE.
LET'S STOP ARGUING AMONGST OURSELVES.
LABOR UNION ELECTIONS - ILDON
SOO-IN LEE

ANYONE ELSE YOU WANT TO NOMINATE?
IF NOT, WE'LL VOTE FOR MR. LEE.
IT'S NO FUN IF THERE'S ONLY ONE CANDIDATE!
WE'LL WANT A RUNNER-UP TO ASSIST, TOO...
I NOMINATE KANG-MIN JU!
HEY!
I NOMINATE HIM, TOO. IT'S MORE FUN THIS WAY!
GO AHEAD!
SOO-IN LEE
KANG-MIN JU

SOO-IN LEE
KANG-MIN JU
WINNER!!

CLACK CLACK CLACK
Fourmis Korea Labor Union - Ildong Branch
ANT BULLETIN
Fourmis Labor Union (Ildong Branch) Officer Elections
The Ildong branch manager must respond to the branch's interview request!
CLACK CLACK CLACK
Store Manager Gaston's Vicious Dismissal Orders
WHAT A WHITE COLLAR GUY.
I WISH I HAD AN OFFICE MANAGER LIKE THIS.
HAVE YOU GIVEN ANY THOUGHT TO WHY YOU LOST?
I'VE ONLY BEEN THERE FOR A FEW MONTHS, AND MR. JU'S BEEN THERE FOR FIVE YEARS...
IT'S DOWN TO BEAUTY!
ELECTIONS ARE ABOUT FACES!

BUT MR. LEE HAS CHARM!
BUT HE COMES OFF AS BROODING. HE SHOULD BE RADIANT!
LOOK AT ME! TELL ME I'M NOT GLOWING!
I DON'T THINK YOU REALLY HAVE ROOM TO TALK ABOUT BEING BEAUTIFUL.
WHAT DID YOU SAY TO ME?!
Fourmis
SQUEAK SQUEAK
쿠르르르르르르....

GOOD MORNING,
MR. PRESIDENT.
AH! HELLO,
UNION MEMBERS!
GOOD
MORNING.
콰직
THUMP

HELLO, EVERYONE.
I'M KANG-MIN JU, PRESIDENT OF THE FOURMIS LABOR UNION.
I KNOW IT'S BEEN A TOUGH TIME AT WORK LATELY.
I'M SURE THE ATMOSPHERE MAKES PLENTY OF YOU WANT TO WALK AWAY FROM YOUR JOBS, BUT THAT'S EXACTLY WHAT THE COMPANY WANTS.
THE COMPANY WANTS US TO LEAVE ON OUR OWN BECAUSE LEGALLY FIRING PEOPLE IS A HASSLE AND A WASTE OF MONEY!
JOIN THE UNION! LET'S FIGHT TOGETHER TO PROTECT OUR JOBS AND OUR RIGHTS!
YOU DON'T HAVE TO SIGN UP RIGHT AWAY!
BUT IF YOU'RE BEING PRESSURED TO LEAVE OR YOU'RE BEING TREATED UNFAIRLY BY THE COMPANY, SEEK UNION REPRESENTATION.
YOU SHOULD NEVER WRITE A RESIGNATION LETTER.
IF YOU HOLD OUT ON RESIGNING, THE UNION WILL PROTECT YOU!

FOURMIS IS EXPANDING INVESTMENT IN THE ASIAN MARKET.
FOURMIS IS EXPANDING ITS INVESTMENTS ACROSS ASIA.
MORE STORES WILL OPEN IN KOREA, AND THEIR SUCCESS WILL DEPEND ON ALL OF US.
WE HIGHLY VALUE EACH AND EVERY ONE OF YOU. OUR COMPANY AND OUR EMPLOYEES WILL GROW TOGETHER.
WELL, HELP YOURSELVES.
MAYBE IT'S BECAUSE HE'S WESTERN. HE HAS GOOD MANNERS, AND HE SEEMS LIKE A NICE GUY UP CLOSE.
RIGHT?
SO WHAT IF HE'S CHARMING? HE STILL WANTS US ALL OUT, NO MATTER WHAT HE SAYS.
DIDN'T HE SAY THAT HE VALUED THE EMPLOYEES?
THEY'LL SAY WHATEVER THEY NEED TO, EVEN AFTER CREATING AND SIGNING OFF ON THE LABOR CONTRACTS.
WOW, YOU REALLY KNOW YOUR STUFF SINCE JOINING THE UNION.

YOU'LL BE REWARDED IF YOU DO A GOOD JOB.
WHEN A NEW STORE OPENS, WHO'S GOING TO HIRE THE STAFF?
YOU'RE GOING TO HAVE TO GO THERE AND MANAGE THINGS.
THE ONLY NEW STORE OPENING NEXT YEAR WILL BE IN ULSAN.
IS ANYONE WILLING TO TRAVEL TO ULSAN WHEN IT OPENS?
FOURMIS HAS SLOWED STORE EXPANSION OVER THE PAST THREE YEARS.
HOW CAN A MANAGER MAKE A COMMITMENT TO A NEW STORE THAT ISN'T EVEN IN THE LONG-TERM PLANS FOR THE COMPANY?

I'M NOT SAYING THIS BECAUSE I'M YOUR BOSS, BUT BECAUSE I'M WORRIED.
DID YOU SEE HOW THEY BOWED TO MR. JU, BUT NOT THE STORE MANAGER?
I DON'T KNOW OF ANYONE WHO HAS BECOME SUCCESSFUL THROUGH JOINING A UNION.
THEY ALL GET FIRED EVENTUALLY.
IT'S ILLEGAL TO FIRE SOMEONE FOR BEING IN A UNION.
NO ONE GETS FIRED FOR UNIONIZING. THERE ARE PLENTY OF REASONS THAT CAN BE FOUND.
AND IT TAKES YEARS OF LITIGATION FOR IT TO BE CONSIDERED WRONGFUL TERMINATION.
AT THAT POINT, YOU'LL BE READY TO RETIRE.
AND DO YOU THINK YOU'D BE ABLE TO KEEP WORKING WITH THE PEOPLE YOU FOUGHT IN COURT?
WOULDN'T THAT BE RIDICULOUS?
EVEN IF YOU FIGHT TOOTH AND NAIL WITH THE UNION, THE PAY INCREASE IS INSIGNIFICANT.
I CAN TELL THE HEAD OF THE SEAFOOD DEPARTMENT TO GIVE YOU A PROMOTION...

YOU'LL GET A PRETTY SIGNIFICANT RAISE WITHOUT HAVING TO LIFT A FINGER.
YOUR KIDS ARE STILL IN SCHOOL, RIGHT?
MR. LEE AND MR. JEONG USED TO WORK TOGETHER IN CHEONSUNG.
MR. LEE THOUGHT HE WAS GOING TO GET PROMOTED RIGHT AWAY. YOU KNOW HOW HE IS.
BUT MR. JEONG GOT PROMOTED FIRST, AND THAT'S WHY THEY DON'T GET ALONG.
...
MR. LEE ONLY DRINKS WITH THE FRENCH BOSSES. NEVER WITH US. DID YOU EVEN KNOW HE DRINKS?

RESIGNING? ALL OF A SUDDEN?
WHAT DID MR. JEONG SAY TO YOU?
NO... IT WASN'T THAT.
EVEN MY HUSBAND THINKS IT'S TIME...
DID YOU HAVE THE RECORDER WITH YOU? DID YOU RECORD THE CONVERSATION?
NO... I WAS TOO WORRIED AND COULDN'T REMEMBER HOW TO TURN IT ON.
I'VE BEEN GETTING ALONG WITH THE BOSS LATELY.
IT DOESN'T SEEM LIKE THE RIGHT TIME.
THAT'S EXACTLY WHY YOU JOIN A UNION!

LATER... I'LL SIGN UP LATER.
SORRY, JOON-CHEOL.
HI, CHANG-WOO!
WHEN DO YOU PLAN ON SIGNING UP?
HEY, CHANG-WOO!
ARE YOU TOO BUSY HAVING DRINKS WITH THE BOSS TO NOTICE ME?
DO I LOOK LIKE SOMEONE ON THE STREET TRYING TO SELL YOU SOMETHING?
IF SOMEONE CALLS YOUR NAME, YOU DON'T ANSWER?!

THAT'S REALLY INTERESTING.
WHAT?
IT'S REALLY HARD TO GET PEOPLE TOGETHER.
YOU HAVE TO STUDY THE LAW, WHICH ISN'T EVEN IN YOUR HANDS...
BUT YOU DON'T HAVE TO TEACH PEOPLE HOW TO PICK SIDES. THEY JUST KNOW.

IT'S...
...IT'S LIKE WE ALL LEARN IT WHILE STILL IN THE WOMB.

*LABOR COUNSELING CENTER

IT'S SOMETHING ELSE TO SEE EVERYONE FALL FOR SUCH OBVIOUS LIES, HUH?
YOU'RE JUST TRYING TO HELP, AND PEOPLE ARE TAKING THE EASIEST ROUTE FOR THEMSELVES.
EXACTLY!
YOU UNDERSTAND WHAT I'M SAYING, RIGHT?
OF COURSE.
THAT'S EXACTLY HOW I FELT WHEN I MET YOU GUYS.
IT'S THAT "SUPERIORITY COMPLEX."
YOU USED TO BE LIKE THEM, BUT THINGS HAVE SHIFTED FOR YOU. AND NOW YOU THINK ***THEY'RE*** STUPID.

I'VE BEEN FIGHTING FOR YEARS, SINCE THE FOURMIS EMPLOYEES FIRST UNIONIZED. WHERE WERE YOU GUYS?
AND WHILE SOO-IN LEE WAS FIGHTING ALONE, DID YOU DO ANYTHING?
DON'T FEEL BAD. IT'S HARD BEING ON THE FRONT LINES.
BUT WHY ARE WE WORKING SO HARD FOR PEOPLE WHO DON'T WANT OUR HELP?
THEY WON'T UNDERSTAND UNTIL THERE'S A KNIFE AT THEIR THROAT.
AND YOU'RE STICKING YOUR NECK OUT UNTIL THE KNIFE IS AT YOURS, RIGHT?
IF YOU DON'T LIKE IT, QUIT. NO ONE IS FORCING YOU TO DO IT.
WHY WOULD WE LEAVE AND GIVE THEM THE SATISFACTION?
WHAT DO YOU REALLY WANT?

REVENGE?
YOU DON'T NEED A UNION TO GET REVENGE.
SAFETY LAWS, FOOD SERVICE LAWS, ANTITRUST LAWS, LABOR LAWS... TAKE YOUR PICK. YOU CAN THREATEN TO SUE AND GO TO THE PRESS WITH ANY OF THOSE.
THE COMPANY'S DIRTY LAUNDRY IS ALL OVER THE INTERNET AND THE STREETS!
AT LEAST THEN YOU CAN HARASS THE BOSSES AND MANAGERS TO DEATH!
IS THAT WHAT YOU WANT? CAUSING THEM GRIEF WILL MAKE YOU HAPPY?
THEN JUST DISBAND THE CHAPTER AND DO IT. WHY PUT PEOPLE THROUGH THE TROUBLE FOR NOTHING?

YOU DON'T HAVE TO BEG PEOPLE TO SIGN UP.
OR TO DRAG THEM AROUND FOR THE SAKE OF FORCING EDUCATION.
BUT IF NEW MANAGERS COME IN WITH THE SAME ATTITUDE, NOTHING CHANGES.
I KNOW.
SO, NO MATTER WHAT YOUR JOB IS, YOU HAVE NO CHOICE BUT TO GATHER PEOPLE AND UNIONIZE.
YOU MAY THINK YOUR PEERS ARE ACTING PATHETIC RIGHT NOW, BUT THEY'RE HOW YOU PUT UP A FIGHT.
WITHOUT THEM, YOU'RE NOTHING.

HOW CAN WE CONVINCE THEM?
SHOW THEM THE BENEFITS OF A UNION.
DON'T JUST SCARE THEM WITH A CRISIS THAT HASN'T HAPPENED YET.
EVERY LITTLE BIT HELPS. FIND SOMETHING SMALL YOU CAN GET FROM THE COMPANY.
WHAT...COULD THAT BE?
YOU'RE THE ONES WHO KNOW YOUR STORE. HOW SHOULD I KNOW?!
AREN'T THERE ANY COMMON COMPLAINTS?
S... SALARY?
YOU THINK YOU CAN ALL GET RAISES?!
FORGET ABOUT MONEY!

DO YOU THINK IT WOULD BE A GOOD IDEA TO SPLIT UP INTO DEPARTMENTS FOR THE EMPLOYEE SURVEY SO WE DON'T OVERLAP?
OH, YES.
I'LL TAKE THE DELI AND THE BAKERY.
YOU TAKE CARE OF PRODUCE. MR. HWANG CAN DO THE SEAFOOD DEPARTMENT...
...AND MR. NAM, DO YOU KNOW PEOPLE IN THE MEAT DEPARTMENT?
YEAH.
CAN WE PLEASE CALL EACH OTHER BY OUR FIRST NAMES? BEING THIS FORMAL IS SO AWKWARD!
AFRAID NOT.
NO WAY, JOSÉ!
HEY, THAT WAS PRETTY CASUAL!
WHAT? **NUH-UH!**
COME ON...

YOU SHOULD USE HONORIFICS DURING UNION ACTIVITIES.
RIGHT, MR. SECRETARY?
HI... ARE YOU FOURMIS EMPLOYEES?
UH... YEAH.
ARE YOU ON YOUR WAY TO SEE, MR. GU?
YES, BUT... WHO ARE YOU?
I'M AN OLD FRIEND OF HIS.
OHH, I DO BEG YOUR PARDON...!
HAHA.
I'VE HEARD A LOT ABOUT YOU. YOU'RE DOING GOOD WORK.

SEE YOU LATER.
Fourmis
GLOVES?
DON'T WE ALREADY HAVE GLOVES?
PLASTIC GLOVES THAT ARE NO GOOD FOR COOKING.
I NEED LATEX GLOVES, WHICH I'VE BEEN PAYING FOR MYSELF.

WE NEED AT LEAST TWO PAIRS A DAY, SO IT ADDS UP.
AND IF WE LEAVE THEM IN A LOCKER, SOMEONE STEALS THEM, AND EVERYONE STARTS ARGUING.
IT'S A REAL PAIN. PLEASE SOLVE THAT PROBLEM.
DEFINITELY! DON'T WORRY!
CAN WE TRY TO GET EXTRA UNIFORMS?
WE ONLY GET ONE. AND IF IT GETS DIRTY, THERE ISN'T MUCH YOU CAN DO.
DO THEY THINK WE HAVE TIME TO CONSTANTLY WASH AND IRON THEM?
THANK YOU!
NO PROBLEM! KEEP UP THE GOOD WORK!

WE ARRIVE 30 MINUTES BEFORE AND LEAVE 30 MINUTES AFTER OUR WORKDAY.
"GETTING IN UNIFORM, CHANGING SHIFTS, AND WAITING TIMES ARE ALL INCLUDED IN LABOR HOURS."
OH, NO! IT'S BEEN 30 MINUTES ALREADY?
WE NEED TO WRAP IT UP HERE.
"AN EIGHT-HOUR WORKDAY SHOULD INCLUDE AT LEAST ONE HOUR OF BREAK TIME. BREAKS SHOULD BE FREELY AVAILABLE TO WORKERS."
CONTRACT WORKERS ARE EMPLOYEES OF ANOTHER COMPANY, BUT MUST OPERATE ACCORDING TO FOURMIS DIRECTIVES.
A CRIME OF ILLEGAL PROCUREMENT.

BOSS, CAN'T YOU HAVE SOMEONE ELSE DO THIS?
THERE IS NO ONE ELSE.
IT'S WORSE FOR YOU TO STAY STILL WHEN YOU'RE PREGNANT. IF YOU EXERCISE, IT WILL MAKE THE BIRTH EASIER.
OH, NOT THERE! DON'T YOU SEE THE STAIN?
"WORKING IN AREAS THAT PRESENT A FALL HAZARD IS PROHIBITED FOR PREGNANT WOMEN."
DID YOU HEAR HOW MUCH OF HER OWN MONEY YEONG-AE HAD TO PUT IN?
IT WAS SO MUCH!
IF A REGISTER IS SHORT, WORKERS OFTEN COVER THE DIFFERENCE WITH THEIR OWN MONEY, OR IT IS DEDUCTED FROM THEIR PAYCHECK. BUT IF THERE IS AN OVERAGE, THEY DO NOT GET TO KEEP IT.
"NO ARBITRARY DEDUCTIONS MAY BE MADE FROM A WORKER'S WAGES UNLESS THE DAMAGES ARE CAUSED BY THE EMPLOYEE."
YOU'RE NOT IN A HURRY TO LEAVE, ARE YOU? YOU SHOULD MAKE ANOTHER BATCH.
신선한 조
"EVEN IF AN ANNUAL SALARY SYSTEM IS IMPLEMENTED, PREMIUMS FOR OVERTIME, NIGHT, AND HOLIDAY WORK MUST BE PAID."

THE WORLD ISN'T PERFECT. SOMETIMES THERE ARE BROKEN TRAFFIC LIGHTS.

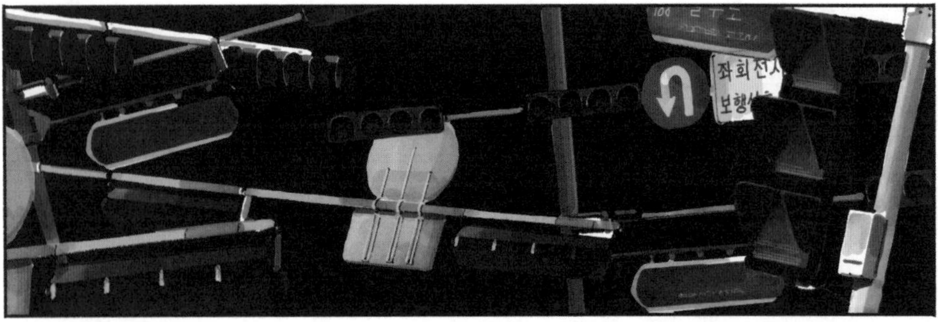

HERE, THOUGH, ALL OF THE TRAFFIC LIGHTS ARE BROKEN.

WHY DO THESE TRAFFIC LIGHTS
EXIST IN THE FIRST PLACE?

Continued in Volume 3.

The Awl

The Awl, volume 2
By Choi Gyu-seok
Lettering: Lynn Eskow
Translation Vibrant Studios

for ablaze

managing editor RICH YOUNG
editor KEVIN KETNER
associate editor AMY JACKSON
designers JULIA STEZOVSKY & RODOLFO MURAGUCHI

This English edition was published by ABLAZE PUBLISHING in 2024 by arrangement with Changbi Publishers, Inc. c/o KCC(Korea Copyright Center Inc.), Seoul and Chiara Tognetti Rights Agency, Milan.

Names: Choi, Gyu-seok, author.
Title: The Awl, vol. 2 / Gyu-seok Choi.
Description: Portland, OR: Ablaze, 2024.
Identifiers: ISBN: 978-1-68497-232-6
Subjects: LCSH Executives--Comic books, strips, etc. | Labor unions--Comic books, strips, etc. | Graphic novels. | BISAC COMICS & GRAPHIC NOVELS / Manga / General
Classification: LCC PN6790.K63 .C4613 A95 2023 | DDC 741.5--dc23